Guns
Of
Vengeance Valley
(Sackett Series Book #7)

Raymond D. Mason

Guns of Vengeance Valley
(Sackett Series Book #7)
Copyrighted © and Published
By Raymond D. Mason
Edited by Lance Knight

Distributed by Kindle E-books

This is a work of fiction. All characters, names, incidents, organizations, and dialogue in this novel are either the products of the author's imagination or are used fictitiously.

You may order paperback copies of books through:
www.Amazon.com
www.bn.com
www.CreateSpace.com
www.Target.com

Or, for personalized autographed copies contact:
RMason3092@aol.com
Or call:
(541) 679-0396

For Editing Services contact Lance Knight by E-mail:
muser4u@gmail.com

For a discount on paperback copies of Mason's books go to www.createspace.com and use the following discount
code at the bottom of the 'Checkout' page to receive a 30% discount: L9ZJ9ZJJ

Preface

After losing his wife, Julia, while making a move by covered wagon to California, **Brent Sackett** considered returning to Texas, but realized he had a responsibility to the others traveling with him who were depending on him to get them out West.

Leaving Las Cruces, New Mexico, Brent, along with Mrs. Cheryl Keeling, Grant Holt and his baby Gracie, Hank and Annie Thurston, and Denver Dobbs headed on towards their next stop, Lordsburg, New Mexico.

Meanwhile, **Brian Sackett**, Brent's identical twin brother, and **AJ Sackett**, the eldest of the Sackett brothers, had returned from Mexico, where they had caught up with two men responsible for the wounding of their father, **John Sackett**. When they returned to the ranch, Brian and AJ learned that someone had poisoned several waterholes on the Sackett ranch and the two brothers set out to find the ones responsible.

John Sackett's nephew, **Lincoln (Linc) Sackett**, the son of **Dave** and **Patty Sackett** , while working on a cattle ranch in Arizona, became good friends with **Clay Butler** when Butler signed on to help break horses that were to be sold to the US cavalry.

Butler was on the trail of three men who had robbed a bank in Cottonwood, Arizona and killed his sister while making their getaway. He didn't know the names of the men, but knew they were all three riding horses that bore the same brand. He had been able to follow the men by the horse's brand to the Pima County area.

When the territorial marshal, **Bud Starr**, began asking questions about the horse's brands identified by witnesses to the bank holdup, **Ike Carter**, the ranch owner the three bank robbers worked for, sent them to **Old Man Clanton's** place on the Arizona/Mexico border until the heat died down. It didn't take long for the men to get bored, however, and decide to move on.

Luther King, Bill Leonard, and **Jim Crane** were the names of the men who had robbed the bank in Cottonwood. They had killed Butler's sister while making their escape. Upon hearing about a silver strike in Nevada from a man they met shortly after arriving at Clanton's ranch the three decided to head north to Nevada. Their journey north, however, would be short lived when they learned of another silver strike in a town recently named Tombstone.

Chapter 1

Old Man Clanton's Ranch
August 23, 1878

'Old Man' Clanton gave the three men standing before him a stern look as they told him their intentions.

"Yeah, Mr. Clanton, we're heading north to Virginia City. There's still a lot of money to be made up there," Luther King stated.

"You boys have stayed here on my ranch eatin' my food, drinkin' my 'drankin whiskey' and not doin' a full day's work for it and now you're just going to pull up stakes and move, huh?" Clanton snapped.

"We paid you a hundred dollars the day we arrived in case you forgot," King growled in a perturbed voice.

"That barely covered my cost of hidin' you boys out. Why, I had to lie like a dog to the territorial marshal when he came nosin' around here," Clanton argued.

"I think that comes pretty natural to you, Mr. Clanton," Jim Crane said, getting an agreeing nod and grin from the other two men.

"No need to say that, Crane. I've been good to you boys and you know it," Clanton said in a sorrowful tone of voice.

"Yeah, you have at that. I'll tell you what Mr. Clanton; we'll give you another twenty dollars, how's that sound?" King said.

"That's better, but forty would sound a whole lot better," Clanton said and spit a stream of tobacco juice off to one side.

King grinned slightly, "Split the difference with you...thirty dollars."

"You said the magic word," Clanton said as King fished out thirty dollars and handed it to him.

King cast a quick glance at his two sidekicks and said with a smirk, "We were ready to give you a hundred if you hadn't gone into that 'woe is me' song and dance."

The three of them laughed as Clanton's face turned red and he swallowed half of the chaw of tobacco he had tucked in his cheek. He began to cough and wheeze and tried to cough up the chaw as the three desperadoes walked towards their horses.

By the time the three men had mounted up, Jonas had managed to clear the chaw of tobacco and started walking towards the hitching rail where the three men's horses were.

"You really were going to give me another hundred, Luther?"

"That's what we had agreed on, but hey, you nixed that deal with your complaining. Now you'll have to be satisfied with the thirty," King replied.

"That's a fine kettle of fish. Here I take you boys in and treat you like you're my own flesh and blood and you go and pull a dirty trick like that. Why, for another ten dollars I'd fight the lot of you...one at a time mind you," Clanton snapped angrily.

Bill Leonard's smile dropped from his face and a frown formed. Leonard was a man with a violent temper and a short fuse that would set it off. King cast a quick glance in Leonard's direction and said under his breath, "Forget it, Bill...we might need him again sometime."

"I won't. I ain't ever coming back to Arizona once I leave," Leonard said as he climbed out of the saddle.

Clanton looked at the dismounting Leonard and began backing towards his house. Seeing that Leonard was about to take him up on his offer, Clanton then looked around the yard quickly to see what he might use as a weapon. He spotted a branding iron propped up against the front steps and quickly grabbed it.

Leonard walked straight towards the older man with a deep set scowl on his weathered face. Jonas pulled the branding iron back in a threatening manner as Leonard drew ever closer.

"You swing that iron at me, 'Old Man', and you'll never see another sunset," Leonard said tightly.

"Wha...," Clanton started to say and then realized he had gone too far with the short tempered Leonard.

Leonard hit Clanton who still held the branding iron back as though ready to swing it. The force of the punch knocked the older man to the ground in a heap. Leonard grabbed Clanton by the front of the shirt and jerked him to his feet. Another crushing blow and Clanton was knocked unconscious.

Leonard reached down and tried to pull the unconscious Jonas to his feet again, but couldn't due to the dead weight of the old rancher. Leonard let go of the front of Clanton's shirt and let him drop back onto the dusty ground. Leonard gave Clanton a short kick to the stomach before turning and walking back to his horse.

Once he'd mounted up King gave Leonard a hard, stern look and said, "You had better hope you never run across Ike Carter after this. He's good friends with Old Man Clanton."

Leonard looked at King and stated, "He'd better hope he doesn't run across me."

The three of them reined their mounts around and headed in the direction of Tucson. After they'd ridden a ways Jim Crane looked over at Leonard and said seriously, "Forget Ike Carter, you'd better hope you never run into Ike Clanton or his boys. He makes 'Old Man' Clanton look like a Sunday schoolteacher. Old Man Clanton is Ike's pappy and pretty fond of the man from what I hear."

"Oh, is that what you hear?" Leonard said sarcastically.

"We're riding wide of the Clanton's place as well as Carter's. I do want to make a stop along the way, though, and say 'adios' to one...Buck Benton; the ramrod of the X-X ranch. He's been a thorn in my flesh for sometime," King said with a frown.

"You mean Buck Benton?" Leonard asked.

"Uh huh; I've got a score to settle with him from several years ago," King stated.

"What about that Linc Sackett?" Leonard snapped.

"He ain't done nothin' to me," King replied.

"He did a number on a couple of the boys, though. If you don't want him, I'll take him," Leonard stated.

"You've got him then. Just keep him off my back," King said as the three of them rode along.

The three rode north along a stagecoach road. They had ridden about five miles when they topped a rise and saw a stagecoach that had lost a wheel on the road ahead. There were three men working at getting the wheel back on the coach.

One of the men was the driver and the other two were passengers, because the man riding shotgun was standing guard. They were in Apache territory and the word was out that a number of Chiricahua had jumped the reservation and had been making trouble for travelers.

As the three riders approached the stagecoach King commented, "That must be the stage for Lordsburg."

"Probably," Crane replied.

King looked over at Leonard and said with a slight grin, "Should we see if we can help these folks out?"

"Yeah...help them out of their money...if they've got any," Leonard said with a laugh.

"Hey, it's a Wells Fargo stage; they very well could be hauling a bulging strongbox," Crane added.

"You two take care of the passengers and I'll take care of the driver and man riding shotgun," Luther King said.

As they approached the coach they noticed that there was a woman standing off to one side and watching the men working on the coach's wheel.

When they were less than a hundred yards away from the coach Jim Crane spoke up.

"Hey, I know that woman," Crane said.

"You do?" King answered. "Who is she?"

Crane grinned, "That's Shelah Colton."

"D'you mean Shelah?" Bill Leonard asked.

"Yeah, and there's Bob Colton," Crane said seriously.

Leonard frowned, "So this is the bad man Bob Colton huh? It'll be a pleasure to take a stagecoach he is a passenger on."

Luther King cast a serious glance in Leonard's direction and said, "You don't think you're any match for Colton do you?"

"I ain't afraid of him, if that's what you mean," Leonard snapped back.

"A number of men weren't afraid of him and they're planted on boot hills all over the territory. I say we pass on this coach," King stated firmly.

"I never knew you to be one to run from a hired gun, Luther," Leonard growled.

"Bob Colton is not just another hired gun. He is one man I don't care to tangle with. If you want to take this coach you'll have to do it without me," King snapped.

"That goes for me too," agreed Crane.

Leonard looked at the two with disgust written all over his face. He shook his head slowly, "I'll be cuttin' loose from you two as soon as we get up to Nevada. I don't want my name associated with cowards."

"I know you, Bill. And I know I can take you any day of the week. Don't think you can prod me...you ain't Bob Colton by any stretch of the imagination," King said with a deep scowl.

"That's still debatable, Luther. You think you can take me...I don't," Leonard said with a steady stare.

"We may have to find that out one day," King replied.

The three men were now alongside the stagecoach and reined their horse to a halt. King looked over at the driver and asked, "You men need any help?"

"No thanks, we've just about got it now. Where are you headed," the driver asked?

"North...up to Virginia City," King replied.

"Aw, you've got the fever, huh?" the man riding shotgun said with a laugh.

"Yeah, you might say that," King replied.

Leonard was eyeing Shelah Colton and she didn't like the way he was ogling her. Although the two had never met there was an instant dislike for one another. Leonard's attempt to stare her down didn't work on this tough lady.

"Once you get your eyes full maybe you'll want to fill your pockets, too," Shelah finally said in a serious tone of voice.

Leonard didn't answer her, merely continued to glare at her. She shook her head slowly and said loud enough for him to hear her, "Poor man...he's deaf, dumb, and stupid."

Leonard started to say something when the man helping the driver and Bob Colton stepped around the corner of the coach and gave him a look.

It was then that Leonard along with King noticed the marshal's badge pinned on the man's shirt under

Raymond D. Mason

his jacket. Leonard and King gave one another a quick look and then looked back towards the marshal.

Leonard fixed his gaze back on Shelah and said in a monotone voice, "I ain't got no use for you so why should I want to fill my pockets with visions of you?"

Shelah started to answer when Bob Colton walked around the corner. He sensed the tension in the air and commented.

"Is he bothering you, honey?" Bob Colton asked his wife.

"No, the poor man is just a little touched in the head; probably been out in this Arizona sun too long. I think he's harmless," Shelah said with a slight grin at her husband.

Bob looked at Leonard for a moment and then said, "I know you. Isn't your name Leonard...uh, Bill Leonard?"

Leonard straightened in the saddle as he muttered, "No, that's not my name."

Colton grinned slightly, "We didn't meet once up around Cottonwood?"

At the mention of Cottonwood Leonard took on a very serious look. Cottonwood was where the bank he and his two cohorts had robbed was located. Leonard didn't answer the question right away, but finally replied.

"No, I ain't ever been to Cottonwood."

"Man, you sure look like a gent I met up that way. What handle do you go by, if you don't mind my asking?"

"I do mind. I ain't ever seen you and you ain't ever seen me," Leonard said tightly.

Colton merely grinned and then glanced at his wife before saying, "Okay, if you insist. You sure look like that fella Leonard, though. Honey, I'll be over here helping get that wheel on if you need me."

"I can take care of myself," Shelah said and gave Leonard a quick glance.

Luther King and Jim Crane rode around to the side of the coach where Leonard was and King said, "Come on, Bill. They don't need us to give them a hand."

"Bill?" Shelah said with a questioning look on her face.

"Bill Smith," Leonard said with a deep set frown.

Luther King looked at Leonard and then quickly towards Shelah and tipped his hat, "Yep, that's his name, Bill Smith...Mrs. Colton! Take care of yourself and have a nice trip to wherever it is you and your husband are headed."

Shelah gave him a hard look and then cast a quick glance to see if anyone had heard what the man had called her. She wasn't sure if there was a wanted poster out on her and/or her husband and they were traveling under an assumed name on this trip.

"Now you've got me mixed up with someone else," Shelah said coyly.

With that King and the other two kicked their horses up and headed north. Shelah watched them ride off and shook her head slowly.

"Now there goes trouble if I ever seen it," she said.

Raymond D. Mason

Chapter 2

Once the stagecoach wheel had been fixed Bob Colton and his wife Shelah climbed aboard. The coach continued on its way to Lordsburg, New Mexico.

One of the other passengers was a Special US marshal by the name of Sam Booker. He was on his way to Lordsburg to pick up a prisoner who was being held by the sheriff there.

The man had escaped from the territorial prison in Yuma and Booker was going to take him back. The Colton's had learned this and were glad they had not planned on robbing this particular stagecoach.

"So what's this man's name you're going to take back to Yuma, Marshal?" Bob Colton asked.

"Jack Yancey. He's a hard case. He killed three men who had helped him rob a freight office up in Tucson and took the money all for himself. A posse caught up to him a few days later. He put up quite a fight from what I heard. Killed three and wounded two posse members; at least that's what I was told anyway," Booker said.

"And you're taking him back by yourself? You're a braver man than I am," Bob said.

"He'll be in chains. I've never lost a prisoner yet, and I ain't about to start now."

"Well, all I can say is good luck," Colton said and gave Shelah a quick glance.

The truth was that Colton knew Yancey and was actually glad to see him in custody. Yancey and Colton had worked together on a couple of jobs and Colton was sure that Yancey was responsible for the sheriff and a posse waiting for them on the last job they pulled together. Fortunately, Colton had managed to get away; as did Yancey. The others involved in the holdup weren't as lucky, however.

"Where did you folks say you were headed?" Marshal Booker asked.

"Well, we're getting off the coach in Lordsburg, but we're actually headed out to California. We're going to take the train into southern California. I've never been on a train before and kind of looking forward to it," Colton lied.

The truth was he had ridden several trains and had devised what he felt was a workable plan for holding one up. Colton would be in need of some help in pulling his plan off though and figured on putting together a gang once he was in California.

The marshal grinned, "It's an experience. I've been on a number of them and prefer them to riding like this. It's a heap more comfortable and not to mention faster."

"So when will you be taking your prisoner back to Yuma?" Colton asked.

"As soon as I can get him chained up; I haven't seen my wife in over two months," the marshal said seriously.

"My goodness; I'll bet she misses you," Shelah said.

"I hope so; I'd hate to think she didn't," the marshal said and chuckled. He then asked, "So what line of work are you in Mister....?"

"Kaufman, Bob Kaufman. I'm in the banking business actually. We deal with various stage lines quite a bit," Colton said and cast a quick look Shelah's way.

"So is this a business trip?"

"Yes, that's why we are headed out to California. We have business out there," Bob said, still being truthful. The only problem was that the 'business' they had was the business of robbing a bank in Monterey, California.

"Have you ever been out to California before?" Booker asked.

"Nope; it'll be the first time for that too," Bob answered.

The conversation dropped off and before long the three of them had dozed off. The easy rocking of the stagecoach had put them all three to sleep. Their sleep was short lived, however. They were awakened by gunshots.

"Over on the right," the driver yelled out loudly as the man riding shotgun spun his Winchester around and leveled it on the Chiricahua leading four others on the right side of the coach.

When the Apache saw the rifle aimed in his direction he leaned off to one side of his horse, making himself next to impossible to hit. The bullet passed over his back. The next shots fired came from inside the coach.

Awakened by the yelling and gunshot, Marshal Booker had pulled his pistol and was firing at the marauding Apaches. It wasn't that the small war party wanted to rob the stagecoach, but rather just kill its occupants.

When Colton joined in the shooting along with the marshal, the attacking warriors were forced to pull away. They had not anticipated the passengers taking up the fight along with the man riding shotgun.

As the occupants of the coach watched the Apaches ride away, Colton remarked, "Man...and I was having such a good dream."

"I'd better have been in it," Shelah said appearing to be very serious.

"You were, honey...you know you were," Colton said and winked at the marshal.

"Do you think they will come back?" Shelah asked, turning serious as she addressed the marshal.

"Only if they can pick up some more braves to join them," the marshal replied. "They thought they'd have an easy time of it. I guess they hadn't figured on the passengers joining in the fight."

"They must be very new at this then," Bob Colton said with a frown.

"They were; you can count on it. This is how the young ones learn about things such as this. 'Experience is the best teacher' is the way many of the elders of the tribes believe," the marshal replied knowingly.

"I'll be glad to get into Lordsburg," Shelah said as she looked out the coach window.

"We should be there in about two and a half, maybe three hours," the marshal said.

"I wish the cavalry would put a stop to these Indian raids," Shelah went on. "I heard they even attacked a train not long ago."

"Oh, yeah, they admire the Iron Horse, but they ain't afraid to go after it. The ones doing the raiding are a bunch of renegades. Most of the tribes are settled on Indian reservations, but these young bucks are hanging onto the old ways," the marshal stated.

"I heard that a Chiricahua Apache named Geronimo has been hitting folks in this area; is that right?" Bob Colton asked.

The marshal nodded slightly, "He's been working along the border mostly. He hates white settlers and Mexicans. But then...I guess I would too if I'd lost my entire family the way he did."

"Oh, who killed them?" Bob asked.

"It is believed to have been Mexicans. While Geronimo and some of the other braves were out of their camp, some Mexicans killed the braves posted as guards and then slaughtered most of the people in the camp. He lost his wife and child.

"That set Geronimo off and he's been a handful ever since. Too bad, too; he had been a peaceful sort of man up until then," the marshal stated knowingly.

Raymond D. Mason

Chapter 3

At that very moment there were two covered wagons pulling into Lordsburg. Brent Sackett, along with Mrs. Cheryl Keeling, and Grant Holt's baby rode in the lead wagon with Grant riding alongside on his saddle horse. Following Sackett's wagon was the one driven by Denver Dobbs and carrying the Thurston kids, Hank and Annie.

"Mrs. Keeling...would you mind taking the baby and the Thurston kids with you while we men are picking up some supplies from the general store? I'll give you some money and you can treat yourself and them to some candy or whatever," Brent said.

"Of course not; would you mind picking up a few things for me," Mrs. Keeling asked?

"No, just tell me what you want."

"I have a list of things we might need for the kids. One thing for sure is some ribbon for Annie's hair. And that single strand of rope I used to tie it up with is giving her fits and it looks so bad," Mrs. Keeling said with a slight smile.

"You've got it," Brent said as he climbed down off the driver's seat. "We'll meet you back here in one hour. That should give us all time to do what we have to do."

Mrs. Keeling handed the baby down to Brent and then she climbed down also. Brent handed the baby back to her and walked back towards Denver Dobbs' rig.

"You kids go with Mrs. Keeling," Brent said and took Annie by the waist and set her down from the wagon to the ground. "I think she might have a surprise for you."

"It wouldn't be a piece of candy would it?" Hank asked with a wishful grin.

"You'll have to ask her; I'm sworn to secrecy," Brent said with his own slight grin.

"After we get our supplies, Brent, how about I buy you and Grant a cold beer?" Dobbs offered.

"You won't get any argument out of me," Brent said.

"Me neither, Mr. Dobbs," Grant said from atop his horse.

"Tie your horse to the hitching rail over there," Brent said to Grant motioning towards the nearest rail.

"We'll hit the general store and see if they have everything we need. If they don't we'll have to try that mercantile down the street there," Brent stated.

"I hope they sell cartridges, I'm a little low on firepower," Dobbs said.

"I am too," Brent agreed.

"The going should be easier from here on, don't you think?" Dobbs asked as they headed in the direction of the general store.

"You said you had been out to California before," Brent replied with a slight frown. "You tell us if it is."

Guns of Vengeance Valley

"I didn't take the southern route; I took the northern route. That is one rough route I can tell you that. I've heard the southern route is a lot easier," Dobbs said quickly.

Brent gave Dobbs a suspicious look. He still wasn't totally convinced that Dobbs was on the up and up with him. The two had gotten a little closer after the run in they'd had with the gang of outlaws just outside of Las Cruces, New Mexico; but, there remained that seed of doubt in Sackett's mind.

Just as they were entering the store there were gunshots fired down the street to their left. Brent stopped and looked in the direction of the gunfire to see if he could spot the shooter.

As his gaze locked on the large sign that read 'Sheriff's Office', he saw a man run out the front door holding a pistol in his hand and looking left and right before finally grabbing a horse that was tied at the hitching rail and swinging into the saddle.

The man kicked his horse into a full run and looking back over his shoulder in the direction of the front door as he rode away. When another man appeared in the doorway holding a rifle, the man on the horse fired two quick shots, dropping the man who had just exited the sheriff's office.

A man standing near Brent and the others who had witnessed the shooting as well, said, "My god...Jack Yancey has escaped."

Brent looked at the man and then back towards the man on the horse just as he rounded a corner and disappeared. He looked back at the stranger and said, "I take it this Yancey is a bad hombre?"

"The worst from what I hear. He'd shoot his own mother if she stood in his way. He's just bad news all around," the man said.

People began running to the aid of the man who had been downed by the fleeing gunman. His wound was to the leg.

As Brent turned to go inside the store he said under his breath, "They'll get him. It's only a matter of time."

Brent opened the door just as a young, pretty woman carrying an arm load of packages was exiting. Brent held the door open for her and tipped his hat.

"Thank you," the woman said as she cast a quick smile at the ruggedly handsome Brent and then asked, "What was the shooting about?"

"Some guy named Jack Yancey escaped from jail. At least that's what that guy over there said," Brent replied motioning towards the man with whom he'd just spoken.

"Oh, no...Jack Yancey is vicious killer," the woman said.

Brent then looked at the arm load of shopping goods the woman was carrying and said, "It looks like you could use a hand, ma'am. May I help you?"

The woman looked surprised at Brent's offer, but didn't hesitate in accepting it.

"If you wouldn't mind," she said. "I only have to go across the street to the café there. Usually the owner of the store here has a boy deliver what I need, but the boy's home with the flu."

Brent took the top two packages that were balanced on top of the large box of cooking ingredients the young woman was carrying and handed them to Grant who was standing by the door. Brent took the heavy box of goods from the woman and then addressed Dobbs.

"Go ahead and start getting what we need. We'll be back directly," Brent said.

As the three of them started across the street, the young woman asked, "Are you folks just passing through, or do you plan on staying around for awhile?"

"Just passing through," Brent answered, "on our way to California."

"I hear it's beautiful out there," the woman said.

"How long have you owned your café?" Brent asked, really just making small talk.

"Ever since my husband died two years ago," she replied and then added, "I had to do something to make a living and since I love to cook a café seemed the way to go."

Brent nodded slowly, "You're a widow then, huh?"

"Yes, my husband died from the fever."

Brent noticed the name over the café window. It read 'Brenda's Kitchen'. He grinned as he looked back towards her.

"I take it your name is Brenda, am I right?"

"Yes, Brenda Dawson," she said with a smile and then asked. "And your name is?"

Brent paused slightly before answering, "Brent Sackett."

"I met someone named Sackett once. A Lincoln Sackett; is he related to you in some way," Brenda asked.

"I have a cousin by that name, but I've never met him. He's the son of my uncle Dave. How'd you meet him?" Brent asked curiously.

"Oh, he ate at my café several times while he was staying here in Lordsburg awhile back. I remember him because he was so polite," Brenda replied.

"You don't know where he went when he left here do you?"

"No, he did say he was working for a rancher over in Pima County, Arizona, though," Brenda answered as they reached the café's front door.

She opened it and Brent and Grant followed her inside. She had them set the goods on a long counter and thanked them both.

"Thank you so much for helping me with my armload of groceries. I'd like to do something for you. How would you like to have a big slice of blackberry pie? Brenda asked.

"We've really got to get back to picking up our supplies, but thank you for your offer," Brent said.

When he looked at Grant he saw the young man licking his lips as he eyed the blackberry pie that was under a glass cover. Brent chuckled to himself and then said.

"Well, maybe my friend here would enjoy a slice of that pie. Otherwise he'll be standing in a pool of slobber and might drown," Brent said with a laugh.

Brenda grinned and chuckled lightly at Brent's comment.

"When you finish with the pie, Grant, come over to the general store. We should still be there," Brent said and then looked at Brenda and tipped his hat.

"It was nice meeting you, ma'am. Maybe we'll be back later and have dinner."

Guns of Vengeance Valley

"I hope so. And thanks again for your help," Brenda said with a warm smile.

Brent started to leave when two men entered the café. One of them had a scar across his neck that he tried to hide with a neckerchief. It looked like a rope might have been the cause for the scar.

"Brenda, we'll have the special," the taller of the two said loudly and with a hint of anger in his tone. "And hurry up about it."

Brent stopped and gave the two men a hard look. They walked over to a table and sat down. The shorter of the two glanced towards Brent and frowned.

"What are you looking at, jaybird?"

"That's what has me puzzled," Brent said tightly. "I ain't sure what it is."

The two men stared at Brent but didn't answer back. Brenda sensed the trouble that might be brewing and quickly intervened.

"Oh, Mr. Vengeance, this is a friend of mine, Brent Sackett," she said looking anxiously at the three men.

Judd Vengeance nodded slowly and then said tightly, "Excuse my friend's comment, Sackett. He's a little sensitive about the scar on his neck."

"I wasn't looking at the scar," Brent replied tightly. "I was just wondering why you were so rude to the lady here."

"Rude? We weren't rude. Brenda knows me and knows that I'm a busy man. I own half this town and working on owning the other half," Vengeance said with more a sneer than a grin.

Raymond D. Mason

"And is this hoss your right hand man?" Brent said motioning towards the shorter man with the scar.

"This man works for me, yes. Maybe you've heard of him; Jack Buell," Vengeance said as if expecting a yes answer.

"I ain't ever heard the name," Brent replied.

"That makes two of us, Sackett. I ain't ever heard that name either," Buell said evenly.

"I'll have that lunch for you right away, Mr. Vengeance," Brenda said with a look of concern still etched on her face.

"No hurry," Vengeance said in a kinder, softer tone of voice and then looked at Brent and added. "Is that better, Sackett?"

"Much better," Brent said and tipped his hat as he walked out of the café.

Chapter
4

Linc Sackett laughed when Clay Butler lifted out of the saddle on the bronc he was busting and landed on the ground in a cloud of dust.

"That ground gets a little hard after awhile, Clay," Linc called out.

"Actually, it doesn't hurt as much once you're body is numb," Clay said as he got to his feet and dusted himself off with his hat.

"How many times does it make for that bronc?" Linc said as he jumped down off the corral fence.

"Three for me and two for you...five in all," Clay said.

"He's a buck jumper all right," Linc laughed as he prepared to take another go at the spirited animal.

"You said it. Look at him. As soon as he throws you he goes over and stands by the fence watching you. He's preparing for the next rider. The number of times he's dumped his rider is just about to go to six, I'd say," Clay said with a chuckle as he took a seat on the top rail of the fence.

Linc waited until the two men on horseback had gotten a hold of the halter rope and he approached the unbroken bronco. One of the horsemen had a hold of the bronco's ear so it wouldn't move while Linc climbed aboard.

Once aboard the black stallion Linc took the halter rope and prepared for another gut jarring ride. This time the horse just stood in one spot and didn't move. Linc was leaning back waiting for the first jump, be it straight up or to one side or the other. The horse was so unpredictable it was hard to prepare.

This time around, the horse just stood there as still as could be. Linc gave it a light kick in the side, but still nothing; another kick, and once again, nothing; causing Linc to cast a quick glance towards Butler.

"Maybe he's winded," Clay called out.

"Do you think so?" Linc replied just as the horse shot straight up and twisted so its belly was pointing off to the right; a move called 'sun fishing'.

The move caught Linc by total surprise and he went sailing into the air. With arms and legs flailing to try and get some sense of balance and land on his feet, Linc didn't quite make it. He hit the ground in a heap. Now it was Clay's turn to laugh again.

"I think he belongs in a Wild West Show, don't you, Linc," Clay called out.

"I think you're right?" Linc replied as he got to his feet.

Linc looked at the horse for a moment as it stood calmly by and looked towards him. He shook his head as a thought crossed his mind. Slowly a grin spread across Linc's face as the thought took root.

"I'm going to buy this horse," Linc said as he eyed the animal.

"You're what?" Clay asked, unsure of what he'd just heard.

"I'm going to buy this horse and make a lot of money off him," Linc said and nodded his head in the affirmative.

"Why in the devil would you want to buy this buck jumper, Linc?" Clay asked in a surprised voice.

"Come Saturday you'll see why," Linc said as he walked towards his friend.

"You're serious about buying him?"

"I am. Like I said, I'm going to make me some money off this bronc," Linc said holding the knowing smile.

"I think you're a little addled from being thrown too many times, but if you're bound and determined to do such a fool thing, who am I to stop you," Clay said with a chuckle.

Just then Buck Benton walked out of the main house where he'd been talking with Miss Shauna. He wore a deep scowl on his face as he marched towards the corral. When he neared the spot where Linc and Clay were standing he called out in a loud, almost angry voice.

"Linc...I want to talk to you," Benton said.

Linc turned and faced his ramrod and noticed the angry look on Buck's face.

"Yeah, what is it, Buck?"

"Butler...you'd better make yourself scarce. This is between Sackett and me," Buck said giving Clay a hard look.

Clay gave Benton a questioning look and then glanced towards Linc. Linc never took his eyes off Benton, but gave Clay a slow nod of the head. Clay walked off so he was out of earshot range.

Buck glanced to make sure Butler was far enough away and then lit into Linc, "You been chasing after Miss Shauna, Linc?"

Linc frowned, "No, I ain't been chasing after her. What makes you ask that?"

"She said you were and she wouldn't lie about it," Benton said harshly.

"No, but she could be mistaken about it, Buck. Listen, she let me know her feelings about me when I made the trip into Tucson to fetch her home. You don't have a problem with me, Buck. You're only problem is with Miss Shauna and her feelings for you...or the lack of them," Linc said bluntly.

Buck's face reddened as his fists clenched in a silent rage. He took a step towards Linc but stopped short when Linc said, "Don't do it, Buck. I won't stand still for it."

Buck clenched his teeth and uttered, "Get off this ranch. I don't ever want to see your face around here again. If I do I'll...," he said stopping short of what he wanted to say.

"You'll what, Buck?"

"...Just get off this ranch."

Linc nodded his head slowly and started to walk to the bunkhouse. He stopped and looked back at Buck and said firmly, "I want to buy that black in the corral. You can hold the price of it out of what I have coming in pay."

Buck looked at the black and then back at Linc and snapped, "You can have it for ten dollars. It ain't no good to us. No one can ride it."

Butler had been watching and when Linc walked away, Clay walked over to him and asked what Buck had wanted.

Guns of Vengeance Valley

"He just fired me," Linc said.

"Buck fired you? Clay asked.

"That's right. I'll see you around, Clay."

With that, Linc walked on to the bunkhouse and started packing up his belongings. While he was in the process of doing so, Butler walked in and went to his bunk. When Linc glanced towards his friend he saw him packing up his belongings, as well.

"What are you doing?" Linc asked.

"I just quit. You ain't going to make all the money off that 'buck jumper' by yourself. I want a piece of that action, too," Clay said with a slight grin although he was very serious.

"You don't even know what my plans are for that horse," Linc stated.

"I think I do. I ain't as dumb as you might think I am. You're going to have guys put up money to see who can ride that bronc, I know. You just might get rich off that jumper."

Linc chuckled, "Yeah and we might starve to death, too."

"Oh...I hadn't thought of that," Clay said pretending to have a new concern.

Luther King, Leonard, and Crane topped a hill and looked down towards the small saloon known locally as 'Muldoon's'.

"There's a welcome sight," King said.

"You can say that again. Let's get down there as fast as we can. I hope he's got something to eat," Leonard replied.

"You don't call what Muldoon serves food do you, Bill?" Crane laughed.

"It ain't that bad."

Raymond D. Mason

"It ain't that good, either," Crane replied.

The three desperadoes rode down the hill and reined up in front of Muldoon's. As they stepped down off their horses a man walked out of the small cantina and stopped when he saw them. It was Whitey Howard Haisley.

"Well, look what blew in off the desert," Whitey said with a half smile.

King looked at him and grinned, "Hello, Whitey. I thought you were pushing up daisies on 'boot hill' somewhere. How've you been?"

"Okay, for a man on the dodge. What brings you boys back up here? I heard you had high-tailed it to the border," Whitey replied.

"We're back. Old Man Clanton is a little too old for us. He wanted us to work like ordinary ranch hands. We don't do that kind of work; you know that. We hire out our guns, not our backs," Leonard cut in.

"Say, Bill. I see you're still as rude as you've always been," Whitey answered.

Leonard gave Whitey a hard look before finally saying, "We're going to tangle one day, Whitey."

"That very well could happen, Bill. We'll I'll miss you after it does happen, you can be sure of that," Whitey said, getting a grin from King and Crane.

Leonard just glared at his old antagonist, but didn't respond. The three of them walked to the door of the small bar, and as they passed by Whitey, Leonard gave him another hard look.

"Where are you headed, Whitey?" King asked.

"I'm heading for Lordsburg to see an old friend, Kate 'Big Jaw'. Remember her, Luther?" Whitey grinned.

"Oh, yeah, I remember her. You'd better watch your money at all times," King laughed.

"Ain't it the truth? I thought I'd head on back to Socorro, New Mexico after I've taken care of business in Lordsburg," Whitey went on.

"Well have a good trip and don't wind up losing your scalp to a bunch of Apaches," King said.

Whitey nodded in agreement and then just smiled and as King and the other two entered the bar. He broke into a light chuckle as he mounted his horse and rode away.

Inside the bar the owner, Muldoon, greeted the three warmly.

"Well, welcome home, boys. The first drink is on the house. How long are you going to be around here?" Muldoon asked.

"Pour the drink you're going to buy us and then we'll tell you," King said getting a laugh from Muldoon.

He poured them each two fingers of whiskey and after they'd tossed the drink down, King said, "We're just passing through."

Muldoon held a serious look on his face and then broke into laughter.

"I thought you were serious for a second there," he then said.

"I was," said King.

"Oh, you weren't kidding, huh?"

"No, why would I joke about that?" King replied.

"I thought you had heard the rumor that old Ed Schieffelin found silver near here. He was hiding out from a bunch of Apaches when he spotted a vein of silver running along one of the canyon walls.

"He went looking for someone to stake him and I guess he found it because they've already started doing some mining. He named his mine Tombstone.

"In fact, the word around here is that we'll soon have ourselves a post office," Muldoon said proudly.

"Really; that desert rat really found silver here, huh? We ain't heard nothing like that," King said taking on a serious look.

"That's the word. This place could be a boom town in a few short months. I might wind up a very rich man, too. You know how miners love to drink. I'm looking for some women to provide feminine companionship also. The next time you see me I may be lighting my cigars with five dollar bills," Muldoon crowed.

King looked at his two partners with a questioning look. They knew what he was thinking and nodded in agreement. Perhaps this area was the place to be just in case there was a silver strike.

All three men knew Ed Schieffelin, but had only thought of him as a hapless, ne'er do well prospector always searching for his fortune. He was one of those 'desert rats' that loved the prospecting life. Maybe, just maybe, he had finally gotten lucky.

Wherever a strike, be it gold or silver, is made men from all over flock to that area. Towns spring up over night and the strike brings with it men from every walk of life. The one kind of man you can always count on being there are claim jumpers, and outright thieves; men who would rather rob miners than do the digging themselves.

This strike, as it would turn out, would bring with it a tough, well known lawman and his brothers, Wyatt Earp. It would also bring an old friend of

Earp's by the name of Doc Holliday. The town's name would be Tombstone.

Raymond D. Mason

Chapter
5

Linc Sackett and Clay Butler rode along a familiar stretch of stagecoach road. When they came to the fork in the road, they reined up. One road would take them to Lordsburg and the other road would take them in the direction of Nogales.

"Which way do we go from here, Clay?" Linc asked with a grin.

"I say we go to Lordsburg. I haven't been there for sometime," Clay replied.

"Lordsburg it is," Linc said.

They reined their horses in the direction of Lordsburg and continued their conversation from earlier which centered on Buck firing Linc the way he had. Linc knew the reason and the reason wore a skirt...most of the time. Clay couldn't get over the way Buck would let his personal feelings get the better of him the way he had done.

"I tell you, something just ain't right, Linc. A foreman just doesn't fire his top hand over something so small. Yeah, he's sweet on Miss Shauna, but it ain't like they're ready to tie the knot. I have a sneaking suspicion that she'll raise holy cane when she hears about it," Clay said as they rode along.

"It was about time I moved on anyway, Clay. I knew if I was ever going to get enough money together to get my own place I'd have to think of a better way than cowboying," Linc said evenly.

"Well, you've got a point there. I ain't ever heard of anyone getting rich by simply roping, herding, mending fences, or branding cattle. Well, they might wind up with some money if the branding involves changing a brand," Clay replied with a grin.

"Yeah, they might make a little money, but if they get caught all the money in the world wouldn't save 'em from dancing on air," Linc said with a grin.

"I guess they all think they'll never get caught. If I don't get a lead on the guys who killed my sister I might start to believe someone can get away with robbery and murder," Clay said as a frown crawled across his handsome face.

"We'll find 'em, Clay...it's just a matter of time," Linc said as he looked from Clay towards the top of the rise ahead of them.

Just as Linc scanned the horizon ahead three men on horseback topped the rise. It was King, Leonard, and Crane. Linc straightened up in the saddle as he eyed the three riders.

"Well, well...what have we got here?" he said to Butler.

Butler followed Linc's gaze, "Can you make out who they are, Linc?"

"Huh uh; they're still too far off for me to get a decent look at their faces. We'll be close enough shortly," Linc replied.

Linc and Clay kept their horses at a nice easy lope and keeping their eyes on the approaching riders. As the two groups drew closer Leonard recognized Linc Sackett and grinned.

"It looks like I won't have to go to the X-X to take care of Sackett...here he comes now. I guess he just can't wait to meet his Maker," Leonard said with a leer.

"Who's that with him, do you know, Jim?" King asked.

"Nope, I don't recall ever having seen the man," Crane answered.

"You keep that peckerwood off my neck while I'm taking care of Sackett," Leonard said casting a hard look at both men.

"Yeah, sure, Bill. I just hope you're up to the task at hand," King said with a shake of his head.

"I am," Leonard snapped.

As the riders approached one another Linc said quietly to Clay, "I don't like these hombres' looks. The one in the middle looks familiar to me. I think he used to work for Ike Carter."

"I'm ready; are you?"

"I was born ready," Linc said and slowly lifted his pistol in its holster to make sure it would come out easily should the need arise.

Leonard locked his gaze onto Linc and figured on waiting until they were no more than twenty feet apart to make his play. Linc and Clay eyed the three men with Linc noticing how intent on him one of the men was; that being Leonard.

Leonard said just loud enough for the two with him to hear him, "When we reach that cactus to the left, I'm taking Sackett out. You take care of the other hombre."

Linc sensed that the three men were going to do something; just what it was...he didn't know. Knowing that one of the approaching men was locked onto him, he figured him to be the one to take out first. When they reached the cactus plant Leonard went for his gun.

Linc's hand moved like lightning and his action caused Clay to go for his gun as well. Linc and Leonard's gunshots sounded so close together it was difficult to tell who fired first. It was evident, however, when Leonard pitched backwards and then fell off to the side of his horse.

Clay's draw was also a blur as he leveled his gun on the other two men. Jim Crane had drawn his gun and gotten one shot off when the slug from Butler's .44 hit him in the shoulder. The second shot hit Crane in the chest, killing him almost instantly.

Luther King never went for his gun, but instead put his hands high over his head.

"Don't shoot, don't shoot," King called out. "This was their play, not mine."

"Who are you and why'd they try to kill us?" Linc called out.

"I don't know. We were short on cash, maybe that's what their reasoning was," King said.

"Didn't you work for Ike Carter at one time?" Linc asked.

"Yeah, but we've been down near the border. Why do you ask?" King replied.

Clay rode up alongside King and looked down at the brand on his horse. It carried the Ike Carter brand. Clay glared at the man and said in a tight, clipped voice, "You were up at Cottonwood several months ago. Which one of you killed my sister?" Clay asked.

"You've got the wrong man, mister. I ain't ever been to Cottonwood," King lied.

"You're lying," Butler snapped.

"I ain't lying. These two were up there, but not me. They came back down here talking about a bank they'd robbed. I had nothing to do with it though," King went on with his lie.

"If you ain't ever been to Cottonwood then I don't suppose you'd mind going up there and lettin' some folks take a good look at your face then, would you?" Clay came back.

"It's a long way up to Cottonwood. Why should I go up there when I ain't done a blooming thing," King answered.

"Look...three men robbed a bank up there and my sister was killed. You're with two men that you just said were two of the ones who robbed it. That would make you the third. Now you're going up to Cottonwood with me, or I'll just take the chance that you're the third man and drop you right here," Clay said with a deep set frown.

"Wait a minute...I know who the third man was, but he split from these two when we decided to go down near the border. I went along because of woman troubles. I have a jealous husband after me and didn't want to get waylaid somewhere," King said, sounding convincing with his lie.

While Clay was questioning King, Linc had gotten off his horse and was checking the bodies of the dead men. He found that both men had over five hundred dollars on them.

"How much money have you got on you?" Linc asked.

"What? Don't tell me you're going to rob me?" King replied.

"Just tell me how much money you have on you?" Linc repeated.

"About thirty dollars," King said, knowing that was about all he had on his person. The rest of his money was hidden in his saddlebags.

"Let's see," Linc demanded.

King began fumbling for the money he had shoved down in his pocket while complaining, "I worked hard to save this money and now you're going to take it off me."

"We're not robbing you...what's your name, anyway?" Linc asked.

"I'm Luther King," King said and then looked down at Butler and said, "I'll tell you who the third man in that bank holdup was...his name is Whitey Haisley. The last I heard he was heading for Lordsburg and then on to Socorro, New Mexico," King said, remembering what Whitey had told him.

Clay eyed King hard trying to read in his eyes whether he was lying or not. King didn't let his eyes move off of Butler's knowing that would be a sure give away. Finally Butler accepted his lie.

"You said this hombre's name is Whitey Haisley?"

"That's the man. He was bragging about getting away clean and the posse never got close to them," King continued.

Butler slowly nodded his head, "And you say this fella is headed for Lordsburg?"

"He is at that. We just ran into him earlier today at Muldoon's," King said truthfully for a change.

"Then you're going to Lordsburg with us and you can point him out to me," Clay stated firmly.

"I ain't got no business in Lordsburg, though," King complained.

"You do now," Clay snapped.

King thought it over and saw a way out of his predicament. He'd get these two to kill Whitey. Something he'd hoped would happen for some time.

"Lordsburg it is then," King finally said.

Raymond D. Mason

Chapter 6

**200 miles north of
San Antonio, Texas**

Earl Rule sat staring across the campfire at the smallish Homer Timmons. They were a good days ride from the town that Timmons heard Brian Sackett say he was from, that being Abilene. Rule wasn't sure he trusted this little bookkeeper who was on the run from the law.

"We should be in Buffalo Gap by late tomorrow evening. Once we get there we'll be able to find the Sackett ranch easy enough," Timmons said as he downed the remainder of his coffee.

"I hope you know what you're talking about, Timmons. If you brought us all the way up here for nothing, it's going to go hard on you. I'll gut you like I would an antelope," Rule said staring at Timmons out from under bushy eyebrows.

"I told you Mr. Rule. I heard Sackett telling Miss Gibbons where the ranch was located. He said it wasn't too far from Buffalo Gap. The way he described it I think it was near that cattle railhead called Abilene.

"Besides, I owe you for getting me out of that jail when you did. If I'd been there when the bank detective arrived I'd have nothing but hard time to pull in Yuma staring me in the face about now," Timmons said with a frown.

Earl Rule stared into the fire; the reddish glow from the flames dancing across his face giving him a sinister appearance. He didn't say anything for several seconds, but finally spoke as if speaking to the fire.

"Sackett took my youngest son. He was the only one of my boys that was worth anything. That boy was a godsend. Everything I did in life was for that boy. Brian Sackett is going to pay with his life for taking Johnny away from me."

Rule's other two sons, Rupert and Cory, who were sitting nearby gave one another a quick glance. Their hurt and disappointment was evident, something that Timmons picked up on immediately. He'd commit this to memory just in case he needed it in the near future.

Suddenly Earl Rule seemed to snap out of his stupor and said forcefully, "Let's turn in. I want to be on the trail early in the mornin'."

"I ain't ready to go to sleep right now, Pa," Cory said in a firm, almost angry voice.

Earl stood up and glared at his son. He didn't say a word as he took the quirt from around his saddle horn. Cory was staring into the fire and hadn't seen his pa pick up the short leather whip.

Earl turned around quickly and began to hit Cory with the whip causing him to cover up his head and fall over to one side.

"Pa, stop it," Cory yelled out as his pa beat him.

After several hard swipes with the quirt Earl stopped and glared at Cory, "You'll not sass me again, Cory Rule. No one talks to me in that tone of voice; and that goes for you and your brother as well. Now you turn in like I told you unless you want more of what you just got."

"Okay, Pa, okay," Cory said as he half crawled towards his bedroll.

"That'll teach you to talk back to Pa," Rupert said with a grin.

"You shut up and go to bed, too, Rupert," Earl snapped.

"Okay, Pa," Rupert said getting up from where he was seated and walking to where he'd made his bed.

Earl turned and looked at Timmons who was still seated on a small rock near the fire. Timmons gave Earl a look and when he saw the scowl on Earl's face he, too, quickly got up and moved to his bedroll.

Buffalo Gap, Texas
12:55 pm the following day

The stagecoach pulled up in front of the Buffalo Gap depot and rocked to a halt. The driver called down to the passengers, "Buffalo Gap, all out while we change horses."

The first man to exit the coach was a local businessman who had been to San Antonio on a business trip. Once he was on the ground he turned and held out his hand to help Terrin Gibbons down out of the coach.

Before disembarking, Terrin looked around at the surroundings. She then smiled as she took the man's hand and stepped down. Terrin was followed by three other passengers. The man riding shotgun on the coach was at the back of the coach getting the passengers' baggage from the boot.

Terrin walked to the back of the coach and pointed out her large carpetbag. The man handed it to her with a smile and asked, "How long are you going to be in Buffalo Gap?"

"I'm not sure. At least two weeks," Terrin replied.

Just then a man's voice called out from behind her, "At least that long."

Terrin turned around and saw Brian Sackett standing there with a wide smile on his face. She smiled warmly back at him as Brian took the large carpetbag from her.

"It's so good to see you again," Brian said, and then asked. "How was your trip?"

"Oh, it was fine. No troubles or delays," Terrin replied still holding the warm smile.

"I was very happy when I got your telegram saying you were coming up here. I'll take you to your sister's place seeing as how your brother-in-law is laid up with a busted leg. I stopped by their place on the way into town and told them I'd fetch you from the stagecoach," Brian said as the two started walking to the buckboard he had driven out from Terrin's sister's place.

"How far is your ranch from here?" Terrin asked.

"It's only about twelve or thirteen miles from your sister's place; a little further from town here. I'll take you out there and let you meet my ma and pa. And, of course AJ is looking forward to seeing you again," Brian said as he set the carpetbag in the back of the buckboard and helped Terrin aboard.

Brian stepped up into the buckboard and took the reins. They drove out of town at a leisurely pace heading northwest towards Terrin's sister's place unaware that at that very moment Earl Rule and his sons along with Homer Timmons were no more than twenty miles from Buffalo Gap.

Brian and Terrin filled one another in on what all they'd been doing since the last time they were together. Terrin was very much interested in everything Brian told her; as he was with what she shared with him.

"Oh, look at that little calf over there, Brian. It's bogged down in the mire," Terrin said as soon as she noticed the little animal off to their right.

Brian turned and looked at the bawling calf. He had donned some of his best clothes, wanting to make a good impression on Terrin. When he saw the concern on her face he couldn't hold back the grin.

"Well, it looks like someone needs to help that little doggie out of that mess he's in. Would you mind holding my hat and coat?" Brian said with a half grin.

Terrin smiled, "No, I don't mind at all."

Brian climbed off the buckboard and removed his hat and coat and handed them to Terrin and then walked over to where the calf was mired. Looking at the muck he glanced back at Terrin before taking off his boots and socks and rolling up his pants legs.

"Here goes," he said under his breath as he carefully waded out into the mud hole.

The calf was buried up to its chest so Brian had to slide his arms down into the mud to get a good hold on the little critter. He picked the calf up and started backing up, but after a couple of steps the calf began struggling to get down which caused Brian to lose his balance.

Terrin let out a shocked cry when Brian's feet slipped causing him to fall backwards into the mud. He hit with a splat. Mud flew everywhere and the calf didn't help matters by kicking with all fours.

Brian quickly jumped to his feet and grabbed up the calf again; this time, however, he didn't waste anytime in getting out of the mire. Once out he set the calf down and picked up a small switch and gave the calf a good swat across its hind end.

"That'll teach you to get stuck," Brian said as he watched the calf trot off towards a small herd of cattle.

Brian looked at his once clean shirt and then down at his muddy trousers. He shook his head as he glanced towards the buckboard and saw the look of shock on Terrin's face. After a few seconds, though, Terrin's shock turned to laughter.

Brian shrugged his shoulders as he slowly made his way back to the buckboard.

"This is all your fault, young lady," Brian said, unable to hold back a grin of his own, "I hope you know that?"

"Oh, I'm sorry, Brian," Terrin said bursting out in laughter.

"Yeah, I can see you're just heartbroken over this," Brian laughed.

"Let me clean the back of your shirt off," Terrin said as she continued to chuckle.

"I don't know that I can trust you behind my back," Brian stated. "I think you and that little doggie had this whole thing worked out between you."

Terrin continued to laugh, but not to a point of being rude. She cleaned as much mud off of Brian's shirt as she could and once finished, Brian took care of cleaning up his muddy pants. The two of them laughed at the whole incident as Brian attempted to make himself presentable to Terrin's sister and her family.

Brian drove on to Terrin's sister's place and smiled as the family greeted her. He carried her bag inside and apologized for his appearance. They all had a good laugh when hearing the story as to how Brian had gotten the mud all over him.

Terrin's sister told him they could remedy the muddy clothes and wrapped an old blanket around him. After having a cup of coffee and peach cobbler Brian told them he'd have to be heading back to the Sackett ranch

"Oh do you have to leave so soon? We thought you might spend the night...we have plenty of room," Terrin's brother-in-law offered.

"No, I really do have to get back. We've got water hole problems that my brother AJ and I are checking out. It appears someone has been poisoning them. We think it might be Comanches, but you never can tell," Brian explained.

Terrin's sister thanked Brian for delivering her little sister to them safely and they said goodbye. Terrin walked Brian out to where he'd left his saddle horse tied at a hitching rail.

The two of them set some plans for seeing one another again and Brian started to climb aboard his horse. He put his foot in the stirrup and it looked like he was going to mount up, but then stopped and looked back at Terrin.

Without a word he removed his foot from the stirrup and turned to face the pretty young woman. She looked into his eyes and the two of them kissed tenderly. When their lips parted Brian grinned slightly.

"That was worth a journey of a thousand miles," he said causing Terrin to smile.

"At least," she said.

"If I don't go now, I won't want to leave at all," Brian said.

"I know...and I wouldn't want you to leave," Terrin agreed.

One more kiss and Brian climbed aboard his chestnut gelding and reined it in the direction of the Sackett ranch. After riding about twenty yards he looked back towards Terrin. She gave him a slight wave which he returned.

Brian knew for certain now...he was in love; and it felt great. He'd finally found a woman he wanted to be with for the rest of his life. He didn't know it, but Terrin was experiencing those same feelings herself.

Chapter 7

Buffalo Gap, Texas
7:45 pm

Later that evening, back in Buffalo Gap, Earl Rule was inquiring as to the whereabouts of one Brian Sackett. He had no trouble finding people who had heard of the Sackett's, but they couldn't tell him exactly how to get to the Sackett ranch.

Timmons finally had an idea and told Earl that he'd ask directions from then on. He changed the question entirely. Instead of asking about Brian Sackett, or the Sackett ranch, he begin asking about a young woman by the name of Terrin Gibbons. The first place he asked the question was in the general store.

"Oh, yeah, I know Miss Gibbons. Her sister Eileen told me just the other day that Terrin was coming to stay with them awhile. I can't recall when she said Terrin was supposed to arrive though. I remember thinking it was supposed to be one day this week," the storeowner stated.

"Maybe you can tell me how to find this woman's sister's place?" Rule asked in his usual hard tone.

"Yep, I can do that. You just head out of town to the northwest and go for about eight or nine miles. When you come to a well traveled trail that leads off to your right, take it. They may have a small sign up there to direct you. That trail will take you directly to the Pullman spread. It ain't a real big spread, but they make do," the owner said.

Timmons looked at Earl Rule and grinned, "Bingo," he said.

"It's too late to go out there tonight; it's gettin' on to near nine o'clock. We'll take us a room and head out there at first light. The sooner we find this Gibbons woman the sooner I'll find Brian Sackett," Earl Rule said with a deep frown.

Rupert and Cory were looking around the store while the owner was busy with Earl and Timmons. Rupert looked around to make sure no one was watching and slipped a new bandana into his pocket. Cory saw him and grinned widely.

Taking his cue from Rupert, Cory stuffed a new shirt under his coat. When Rupert saw this, he wasn't about to be outdone by his younger brother, so he moved over to where the belts were hanging. He turned his back so no one could see what he was doing and slipped his old worn out belt off, exchanging it for a brand new one.

About then Earl looked at them and motioned for them to follow him and Timmons out. The two Rule brothers giggled like school kids as they moseyed out the front door with their bounty. Earl noticed and cast a hard glance at both of them.

Once outside Earl turned and addressed his two sons, "Okay you two...what's so funny? You're both grinning like egg suckin' dogs."

"Look what we got while you were talking to that old boy in there, Pa," Rupert said showing his pa the items he'd stolen.

Cory grinned as he pulled out his stolen shirt and proudly displayed it as well. Earl Rule looked at the items and shook his head slowly.

"I've raised a couple of no good thieves. You take a chance on getting caught for stealing over a couple of trinkets like that. How many times have I told you if you're going to steal something make it something worth having to kill someone or going to jail over? This is kids play and it sure ain't anything to be proud of. Now let's find us a hotel room for the night," Earl snapped with a look of shear disgust on his weathered face.

The four men found a hotel and got two rooms. Earl and Rupert stayed in one and Timmons and Cory stayed in the other one. Being older, Earl Rule was tired and went to bed right away. Rupert lay down, but didn't go to sleep.

Rupert waited until his pa's snoring told him he was sound asleep and then slipped out of bed and got dressed. He had spotted a saloon that had a couple of women working a sporting house above it and wanted to pay them a visit.

Not wishing to awaken his pa, Rupert waited until he was in the hall outside the room to put on his boots. As he was doing so Timmons and Cory exited their room.

"Is Pa asleep?" Cory asked quietly.

"Sleepin' like a baby only snoring a lot louder," Rupert said getting a snicker out of his younger brother.

"Then let's whoop it up, big brother," Cory said and the two of them said restrained the urge to laugh out loud.

The three men headed for the Oxtail Saloon that Rupert had spotted earlier. The barroom wasn't all that big, but it did have a man playing piano and there were a couple of 'ladies' working the patrons.

Rupert spotted a large bosomed woman named Lucy who was wearing a very low cut blouse; instantly taking up with her. The two of them took a table near the back of the saloon.

What Rupert didn't know was that she had been with a man by the name of Cleave Taber earlier and he'd gone off to the outhouse which was located in back of the saloon. Cleave Taber was one of the baddest men in the Buffalo Gap area.

Cory and Timmons were at the bar and both men were eyeing a poker game going on at the rear of the bar. Timmons was a pretty good card player and Cory could cheat with the best of them.

"What do you think, Homer? Should we get in that game and see if we can't take them boys for a few dollars?" Cory said with a grin.

"Are you good at cards, young Cory?"

"I'm the best I've ever seen," Cory grinned.

"What do you have in mind?" Timmons asked.

"I'll set you up with a good hand every third hand or so. I'll win a hand every now and then. If I'm the one dealing they'll never think I would be setting it up for you to win and we can take them boys for a good amount," Cory said evenly.

"What are we waiting for? Let's see if they'll let us join them," Timmons said.

Guns of Vengeance Valley

Cory walked over first and asked if he could join the card players. The three men at the table eyed him suspiciously and then all agreed to let some fresh money set in. Timmons waited until Cory was seated and then he, too, asked to sit in and was also allowed in the game.

After about five minutes Cleave Taber reentered the saloon and when he saw Lucy sitting with Rupert clenched his big fists before heading in the two's direction. When he walked up to the table he stopped and just glared at Rupert.

Rupert looked up with a scowl at the huge man standing next to him and asked angrily, "What do you want?"

"You're in my seat and with my woman," Cleave stated firmly.

"I don't see your name on this seat anywhere and I think the woman will be with whoever she wants to be with; who is me, right now," Rupert said.

"Yeah, Cleave, I'll take care of you later," Lucy said.

"You'll take care of me right now," Cleave said and picked the chair up that Rupert was sitting in and carried it, as well as Rupert to the front door of the saloon and tossed the chair and its occupant out onto the street.

The chair hit the ground with a thud with Rupert still seated in it. When it tipped over it spilled Rupert out onto the ground. Two men outside saw what had happened and began to laugh.

Rupert sprang to his feet and pulled his pistol out before rushing back inside the saloon. It was obvious he didn't expect to meet Taber face to face, but he did. Before Rupert knew what had happened,

59

the big man hit him in the face with a massive fist that knocked Rupert out cold.

Cory saw what had happened and rushed to help his brother. Leaping into the air, Cory landed on Taber's back and grabbed him around the head, covering the giant of a man's eyes with his hands.

Taber began to spin around and reached up towards his passenger and grabbed a hand full of hair. With a might tug, Taber managed to flip Cory over his head and onto the barroom floor. Cory lay flat on his back staring up at the big man and for a moment all he saw was the foot being raised to stomp him in the face.

Cory closed his eye and tried to shield his face with his arms. The next thing he heard was the loud roar of a gunshot. Cory opened his eyes and looked up. When he didn't see the man he'd leaped on he raised his head and saw Taber's body stretched out on the floor in front of him.

The next person that Cory saw was his pa, Earl Rule. The smoking .44 in the old man's hand told Cory all he needed to know. Earl had shot and killed the big man.

Rupert began to come around, but before he was fully conscious Earl began to beat him with the quirt he always carried with him. Cory didn't move, sensing that his whipping was coming next.

"Get up you whelp and get back to that hotel room and get our belongings together. You've made it impossible for us to stay here tonight; not after me having to kill this man to save your hide," Earl snapped angrily at Rupert.

Cory was eyeing his pa with fear and trembling. Earl walked over to where Cory lay and extended his hand. Cory looked at his father for a moment and then took Earl's hand.

He expected to receive the business end of the quirt, but instead got a smile from the old man. Cory looked confused as he asked, "Ain't you going to give me a whipping too Pa?"

"Why would I give you a whipping, Cory?" Earl asked. "You tried to help your brother. He's the one who lost the fight and got knocked out cold."

Cory looked at his brother and then back at his pa and said, "Oh, yeah, that's right."

The four of them hurried back to the hotel room and grabbed up their meager belongings. As they departed the hotel, however, Earl helped himself to the money that was kept in a strongbox behind the counter. Of course he had to render the hotel clerk unconscious to do so.

Earl Rule took the lead as his sons and Homer Timmons rode in the direction of the Pullman ranch. They found it with no trouble. When they arrived Earl sent Timmons, Rupert and Cory up to the front of the house. Earl rode around to the back of the house where he was less likely to be seen.

Timmons dismounted and started up to the front door. He was met by Sam Pullman who was holding a double barreled shotgun under his arm.

"What do you want at this time of night?" Sam asked.

"Howdy, sorry to bother you," Timmons said, stopping short when he saw the armed man. "Could you give me some directions to a friend of mine's place? I'm afraid I took a wrong turn somewhere."

"I might be able to. What's your friend's name?" Pullman asked.

Raymond D. Mason

Just then Terrin walked to the door and when she saw Timmons called out excitedly, "Sam that's the man I told you about...the Comanchero."

Before Sam could raise the shotgun Earl Rule called out from the side of the house, "Drop that scattergun or die where you stand. We're looking for Brian Sackett."

Chapter 8

Lordsburg, New Mexico

Brent Sackett drove the covered wagon down bank and off the trail into a grove of trees where there was a small creek. Denver Dobbs followed along behind in his wagon. When Brent stopped, Dobbs pulled up alongside and stopped also.

"This is a good spot, Brent. It's a sight better than the place we stayed last night. We were a little too close to town and that whooping and hollering kept me awake for a couple of hours," Dobbs said.

"We'll make camp here for a couple of days and give the horses a good rest. I don't think we should go on for at least two maybe three days," Brent said.

"I agree, Brent. My team is mighty weary," Dobbs said with a nod.

"Can we go for a swim in that creek?" Hank Thurston asked.

"I don't see why not, Hank. But go down stream a ways," Brent said. "I don't know if it's really deep enough to swim in, though."

"If we can just get wet it will be enough for us," Hank said as he and his sister jumped down off

Raymond D. Mason

Dobbs' wagon and headed in the direction Brent had pointed.

"Be careful," Mrs. Keeling called after the kids.

"Mrs. Keeling will you get some water from the creek and make a pot of coffee? I'm dying for a cup," Brent asked politely.

"I sure will. I'm sure we could all use a cup. While you're setting up camp I'll build a campfire," Mrs. Keeling said.

"Dobbs I want to talk to you before we set up camp," Brent said seriously.

"Sure thing, Brent," Dobbs said with a slight look of concern on his face.

The two of them walked around in back of Dobbs wagon and Brent glanced at Mrs. Keeling who was walking down to the creek with Grant Holt. Brent looked back at Dobbs and spoke candidly.

"I think we should wait here in Lordsburg for at least a week. I talked to a man who said that there's been some trouble with some renegade Chiricahua in the area. They've been hitting small wagon trains heading for California. I'd like to wait until the cavalry has had a chance to chase the band out of the area," Brent explained.

"Okay, that's fine with me. I ain't hankering to lock horns with any Apaches. Are you going to tell the others about it?" Dobbs asked.

"No, I don't think so. If they hear it from someone else I'll just act surprised. I'll come up with some excuse for sticking around here longer," Brent said.

"I'll do the same. Just tell me what your excuse is and I'll go along with it," Dobbs said with a nod.

"Okay. Let's get camp set up and then I'll go out and see if I can kill some camp meat for us," Brent said.

The two men, with the help of Grant Holt set up camp while Mrs. Keeling fixed coffee and began gathering wood to keep the fire hot for the evening meal. Brent rode off to see if he could kill a deer or an antelope. He'd been gone about an hour when four men rode into camp.

"What are you doing here?" one of the men asked with a scowl on his face.

"We're just camping for a few days," Dobbs answered. "Why?"

"I'll ask the questions here; you just give me the answers to them," the man snapped back. "This is Judd Vengeance's range land and we don't want any nesters thinking they can settle in here," the man went on.

"We're on our way to San Francisco; we aren't nesters," Dobbs said holding a steady gaze on the man.

"That remains to be seen. You just make sure you're off Mr. Vengeance's land within three days. Any longer than that and it could spell big trouble for you," the man snapped.

Brent rode up behind the four men and heard enough of what was being said to make his blood run cold. The incident reminded him of what had happened to Julia the day he found her half dead and a rage began to build inside him.

"You go and tell Mr. Vengeance that we'll leave here once we've taken care of our business and not one day before. You heard what my friend said, now go back and tell that to Vengeance," Brent said with clenched teeth.

The four riders had not heard him approaching and turned around quickly to see who had spoken to them. Brent was carrying his rifle and had a dead antelope on the back of the horse he was using for pack.

"Oh...and just who are you?" the spokesman for the others asked.

"The one who will drop you where you sit if you make a play for that gun on your hip," Brent said.

"You don't really think you can take all four of us, now do you?" the man asked.

"No, but I can get two of you and he will take one, as will my friend there in the wagon," Brent said nodding towards Dobbs who had pulled his coat back so he could draw his gun easily enough. Grant Holt was in the back of Brent's wagon holding a .44-.40 on the men.

The four men took stock of their situation and the spokesman said with a head nod, "You make your point clear enough. We'll inform Mr. Vengeance of your plans, but if he doesn't go for it you'll see a lot more riders next time," the man said.

"Bring plenty of shovels then; you'll need 'em for burying your own," Brent answered back.

One of the other riders stared hard at Brent and then a smile broke across his face. Brent noticed and turned his attention towards the man.

"I thought I recognized that voice," the man said. "You're Brent Sackett. We served together in the War," the man said and then added. "Joel, Joel Holbrook."

Guns of Vengeance Valley

A grin came to Brent's face once he recognized the name as well as the man.

"Joel, how've you been?" Brent asked.

"Good, good...and you?"

"Okay as far as okay goes. We're on our way to California, but I guess you know that now. We ain't planning on staying here for long," Brent said, lowering the rifle he had aimed in the men's direction.

"He's okay, Ben. This is an old friend of mine from the War. You've heard me speak of Brent Sackett and some of our experiences. Well, meet the man himself," Joel said.

The spokesman of the riders, Ben Wallace, continued to hold a hard look on his face as he said, "I thought you'd be ten feet tall, Sackett. The way Joel here spoke about you, we thought you were half man and half wildcat."

"Joel always did exaggerate," Brent said and grinned towards his old friend.

"I'll fix it with Mr. Vengeance, Brent. But, let me warn you. Stay out of what is called 'Vengeance Valley'. Mr. Vengeance doesn't want anyone coming through the valley," Joel stated.

"Where is it?" Brent asked.

"You'll know should you come to it," Joel said and gave the other riders a quick look. They all nodded in agreement.

"You boys go on back to the ranch," Holbrook said to the other three riders, "I want to talk to my old sidekick, Brent, awhile longer."

Wallace, still unsmiling, nodded slowly and said, "Don't be too long. We've got other business to take care of in case you forgot."

"I won't. I'll be along directly," Holbrook said.

The three riders reined their horses around and headed back to the Vengeance ranch house. Holbrook and Brent talked for a few more minutes before Holbrook finally said he had to get going.

Joel gave Brent one last warning before leaving though, "Be careful of Judd Vengeance, Brent. He's a man who takes no prisoners...if you get my drift."

"I don't think I'll have any reason to get to know the man, Joel. Not if he leaves me alone, that is," Brent replied.

Holbrook grinned, "Same old Brent. If you're going to be around Lordsburg awhile I'll see you again. Maybe you can buy me a beer," Joel said.

"Or you can buy me one," Brent grinned.

The two men shook hands and Holbrook headed in the direction the other riders had gone. Brent watched him ride away and then looked at the members of his party.

"Help me get this antelope ready for supper," Brent said as Dobbs and Holt walked up to where he was still astraddle his horse.

"Whew, that was close," Holt stated.

"Worried, were you, Grant?" Brent asked with a grin.

"A little," Grant said getting an agreeing nod from Dobbs.

"Don't feel bad," said Dobbs, "I was too."

Brent didn't say a word, merely smiled at the two as he stepped down off his horse. Brent had a gut feeling that they hadn't heard the last of one Judd Vengeance and he was curious as to what was so special about a place called 'Vengeance Valley'.

Chapter 9

Lordsburg, New Mexico

Lincoln Sackett and Clay Butler delivered Bill King to the sheriff in Lordsburg and took a room in the best hotel in town. The sheriff had a wanted poster on King and was holding him until he got an answer from the sheriff in Cottonwood, Arizona.

Linc looked at the man behind the counter in the print shop and asked, "How much will it cost to have some handbills made up? Say, oh...a hundred of them."

"You just want them in black ink, I take it?" the man replied.

"Yeah, I don't want a work of art. Black will be just fine," Linc grinned.

"That'll run you one dollar," the man said.

"A whole dollar," Linc replied.

"A whole dollar, the man parroted.

"Okay, a dollar it is then. Pay the man, Clay," Linc said seriously before breaking into a grin.

Clay looked at his sidekick and shoved his hand in his pocket, fishing out a half dollar.

"There's my fifty percent," Clay said as he tossed the coin on the counter.

Linc chuckled as he laid a dollar on the counter and picked up the half dollar.

"The handbills will be ready in about two hours," the man behind the counter stated.

"Okay, we'll be back," Linc said and he and Clay turned and walked outside onto the boardwalk.

"How about a little poker while we wait," Linc said.

"I hope you're going to play better than you did in the bunkhouse," Clay teased.

"Hey, that bunch of waddies didn't have any money. Why would I want to waste my talent on them," Linc replied.

The two headed across the street towards a saloon. When they entered the first person they saw standing at the bar was the sheriff. He was talking to another man, a man named Jake Buell.

"There's the sheriff," Linc said. "I thought they said that Jack Yancey escaped from jail a couple of days ago?"

"That's the word around town. Why?" Clay asked.

"Wouldn't you think the sheriff would be out huntin' him?"

"Yancey probably headed for the Arizona border. He's their problem now," Clay replied.

"You're probably right."

"I'm always right; you know that, Linc," Clay said in a serious tone which brought a chuckle from Linc.

Linc saw a game going on at a table with only three men seated at it. Linc motioned towards it and the two of them headed that way. When they got

Guns of Vengeance Valley

within earshot they heard one man say, "I think I've got you this time, Mr. Vengeance."

"That's what you said last hand," Judd Vengeance replied.

"Mind if we sit in," Linc asked when they walked up to the table.

"You couldn't afford it, cowboy," Vengeance said tightly.

"Oh, a high roller's game, huh?" Clay replied.

"Far too high for the likes of you," Vengeance said gruffly.

Linc glared at the man, "I'd be careful insulting a man you don't know. It could get you hurt real bad," Linc stated with a frown.

Vengeance looked up into the face of the man he'd just put down. His eyes darted over to Clay Butler's face then and he grinned.

"Oh, I didn't mean it as a slur. Just that you cowhands have got to learn your place. I'm Judd Vengeance. This man to my left is the Lordsburg Cattlemen's Bank president. The man on my right owns this saloon and another one down the street."

"Well, it just so happens that my friend and I are owners of one of the greatest bucking horses that ever dumped its rider. We've got money we ain't even spent yet," Linc said, getting an eye rolling grin from Clay.

"Money you ain't even spent yet...that's rich," Vengeance said shaking his head and then added. "It'll cost you a hundred just to get in the game."

Linc nodded knowingly and then said, "We'll be back after we've had a bite to eat."

"I thought that might turn you away," Vengeance said getting a chuckle from the other two in the game.

"Come on, Clay; let's go and get our money," Linc said as if they had it.

"Yeah, get some of that money you ain't even spent yet," Vengeance said getting a loud laugh from the men at the table.

As Linc and Clay walked away Clay said under his breath, "What did you say that for?"

"What?"

"Money we ain't even spent yet," Clay said closing his eyes and shaking his head.

"I thought it was clever," Linc said shrugging his shoulders.

As they walked up to the bar, Jake Buell eyed them before asking them the question, "What did you want with Mr. Vengeance?"

Linc looked at him replied, "We just asked if we could sit in on the game. Why?"

"Let's just say that I'm his right hand man. That would make me his gun hand man, if you get my meaning?"

"I get it. If we ever have a reason to care about you being his 'gun hand' I'll let you know," Linc answered tightly.

The sheriff who was standing next to Buell entered into the conversation, "I sent a telegram off to Cottonwood asking about that hombre you brought in. I'm waiting for a reply. So you think he might have been involved in a bank hold up, up that way, eh?"

"I think so," Clay said.

Buell continued to glare at Linc which didn't set well with the tall cowboy. Finally Linc responded to the look.

"What's your name, hoss?" Linc asked.

Buell didn't answer right away, but finally muttered, "Jake Buell...does the name sound familiar?"

"No, should it?" Linc replied.

"It should. If for no other reason than to keep you out of harm's way," Buell said.

"Harm...is Joe Harm back in town?" Linc said, making a joke out it.

Buell didn't laugh, but Clay chuckled.

"Come on, Linc. Let's go get a bite to eat and then pick up those handbills," Clay said evenly.

"Yeah, okay. I don't think there's anymore to be said here," Linc replied.

"You've got that right, leather buster," Buell said which brought a grin to Linc's face.

"Speaking of which...we have a horse that we'll bet no one in Lordsburg can ride for ten seconds. Want to bet on it...Buell?"

"I won't try to ride it, but I know a man who will not only try, but he'll ride it," Buell snapped back.

"Bring him around, it's only a five dollar entry fee and a chance to win fifty," Linc said, getting a questioning look from Clay.

"Get the money ready and I'll bring the man into town with me tomorrow," Buell stated.

"We'll be here," Linc replied.

With that Linc and Clay left the saloon and headed for Brenda's Café. When they entered Brenda was waiting on a table and didn't see them before they had sat down at a table near the window.

When Brenda turned around and saw her two new arrivals she started towards them. A big smile came to her face when she recognized Linc.

"Well, I'll be...Linc Sackett. What brings you back to Lordsburg?" Brenda said holding the smile.

"I'm a businessman now. This is my business partner, Clay Butler," Linc said and then added. "This woman is the best cook I've met, other than my ma, that is. I have to say that or Ma will give me a good switchin' if she hears about it," Linc said with a laugh.

"What can I get for you two...businessmen?" Brenda asked with a chuckle.

"What's the special today?" Linc asked.

"Same as it is everyday...beef stew," Brenda said.

"That's what we'll have then," Linc said, "and plenty of that good smelling coffee. Oh, and some corn bread.

"It comes with the beef stew," Brenda smiled.

Linc and Clay talked about their plans for distributing the fliers announcing their challenge to the cowboys who would be willing to put up five bucks to ride their bucking horse.

"I'll take one side of the street and you take the other and we'll hang 'em on every building and give them to everyone we meet on the street," Linc said.

"You know, Linc, this might turn out to be a real good deal. I ain't seen a cowboy yet that didn't think he could ride just about anything that bucks," Clay stated.

"Yeah, they ain't like us are they? We know we can be bucked off," Linc grinned.

"I've got the bruises and scars to prove it," Clay said.

Just then two young women entered the café and found a table near Linc and Clay. Clay glanced towards them and then did a double take. One of the young women saw his reaction and gave him a closer look as well.

"Clay...Clay Butler? Is that really you?" the young woman said.

"Ellen Meyers, well I'll be. How are you doing?" Clay exclaimed.

"Fine, just fine, but my name is not Meyers any more. It's Ellis," Ellen stated and held up her left hand pointing to the ring on her third finger.

"You and Alvin finally tied the knot, huh?" Clay said with a wide grin.

"Last March. We live here in Lordsburg. What brings you to town?" Ellen asked.

"I went into business with this fella. We're in the process of raising bucking stock for rodeos," Clay said getting a wide eyed glance from Linc.

"We've expanded our operation," Linc said under his breath.

Clay and Ellen talked for a few minutes and then Brenda brought their food. When she set the tray down she remembered her discussion with Brent Sackett.

"Oh, by the way, Linc; a fella stopped in here who said he was a cousin of yours," Brenda stated.

"Is that right? What was his name?" Linc asked.

"Brent Sackett, do you know him?"

"Yeah, well, I should say I know of him. If I ever saw him I was too young to remember. I've heard the name, though," Linc said.

"He said the people he's traveling with will be in town for a few days, so you'll probably run into him.

Tell me where you're staying and I'll pass it along if I see him," Brenda said.

"We're staying at the Lordsburg Hotel. I'd like to see him," Linc replied.

"Okay, I'll tell him," Brenda replied before turning and taking Ellen and her friend's orders.

Chapter 10

Buffalo Gap, Texas

Earl Rule, along with his two sons, and Homer Timmons sat at the Pullman's dinner table gobbling down their platefuls of fried eggs, bacon and hot biscuits. They kept a wary eye on the members of the Pullman family; including Terrin and the two hired hands the Pullman's had working for them.

The Pullman's and Terrin didn't eat with the others, merely watched their captors. Earl Rule looked up from his plate; first at Sam Pullman and then at Eileen and Terrin.

"You're a right fine cook, woman," Earl said to Eileen. "You're a lucky man," he then said turning his attention towards Sam Pullman.

Sam merely nodded his acknowledgement, causing Rule to turn his attention towards Terrin.

"So when do you expect Sackett to come back here to see you? I know he will, because Timmons told me the two of you are sweet on one another," Rule said.

"I have no idea when he will be back this way. He may not even come back while I'm here. He said they've got a problem on their ranch; someone is poisoning their waterholes," Terrin said tightly.

"Is that right? Well, I say he will come back here because that's the reason you came to Buffalo Gap. It wasn't to see your sister, it was to spend time with this Brian Sackett," Rule said wiping his mouth with the back of his shirt sleeve.

Rule looked at Timmons who was just finishing his breakfast and said, "Go out and check the road. I don't want Sackett riding up on us unannounced," he ordered.

"I thought I'd have another cup of coffee," Timmons complained.

"Take it with you," Earl said firmly.

Timmons didn't argue, he had learned it was not the smart thing to do. He got up, poured himself another cup of coffee and went out to watch the road.

Terrin glared at Rule and snapped, "Brian told me about your son, Mr. Rule. He didn't want trouble with your boy, but he had to shoot him in self defense. Your son wouldn't back off and drew his gun first."

"That's a lie, madam. My son was shot down in cold blood by that murdering Brian Sackett and I'll not rest until I see his bones bleaching in the sun. Do you hear me, young lady?" Rule said angrily.

"I feel sorry for you. You're old and bitter and your heart is filled with nothing but hate for anyone and everyone who crosses you. You'll die old and miserable and totally alone," Terrin stated.

Earl Rule stiffened at her words. He wasn't used to anyone talking to him in this manner and certainly not a woman. His eyes grew wider with each of her words until finally he roared.

"Shut your mouth woman! No woman can talk to a Rule the way you just did and not receive a whipping for it," he said!

Turning to Rupert, Earl said, "Take her outside and tie her to the hitching rail in front of the house. I'll teach her a thing or two about manners."

Rupert grinned as he looked from his father to Terrin and then over to Cory.

"Come on Cory, you can have some fun too," Rupert said.

The two of them got up and started towards Terrin. She looked from one to the other as she stood up. When they got to within about four feet of her she grabbed up a fork and pointed it at Rupert.

Rupert grinned and feigned a charge at her. Terrin took a swipe at him with the fork, but didn't come close to catching him with it. Cory moved in and Terrin took a swipe at him as well. The two brothers giggled as if playing a vicious game.

When they both rushed her at once Terrin was able to jab Rupert in the stomach with the fork. The force with which she jabbed at him, coupled with the speed he moved was enough for the fork to sink at least a half inch into his belly.

Rupert backed up and looked down at the fork sticking out of his stomach. Cory had grabbed Terrin by the hair and then wrapped his arms around her. Rupert looked towards his pa and then at Cory.

"She cut me...she cut me," he said as he once again looked at the protruding fork.

"Give her a good 'what for', Rupert," Earl said. "You can have the honors of laying the whip to her back."

Rupert pulled the fork out of his stomach and placed his hand over the punctured area. When he pulled his hand away he had blood on it. He slowly turned his full attention towards Terrin.

"I'll lay your back wide open, woman," Rupert growled.

He and Cory literally dragged Terrin outside to the hitching rail and tied her hands to the cross rail. Rupert moved around where he could get hold of the back of her dress and ripped it off her back.

Earl Rule had followed the boys outside and when Sam Pullman and one of the hired hands got out of their chair, Earl pulled his pistol and aimed it at them.

"Cory, you keep an eye on the others while Rupert teaches this woman a lesson," Earl said.

"Aw, Pa, I want to watch," Cory complained.

"Do as you're told or I'll give you the same thing she's about to receive," Earl snapped.

Cory complained but not too loudly. Earl removed the quirt that he always carried with him and tossed it to Rupert.

"Do what needs to be done, Rupert," Earl said.

Rupert slipped the loop over his wrist and drew the quirt back to strike Terrin's bare back. Before he could unleash the blow, however, a shot rang out that hit Rupert in the shoulder.

The force of the bullet spun Rupert completely around causing him to lose his balance and fall to the ground. When Rupert collected himself enough to go for his pistol, another shot rang out hitting him in the chest. He fell backwards and didn't move.

Earl Rule looked towards the side of the house where the shots had come from only to receive a Comanche arrow in the stomach. He looked down at it and then raised the gun and fired at the Indian that had shot the arrow, killing him instantly.

Before Rule could get back inside the house another arrow struck him in the back. Rule staggered forward still attempting to get inside the house. A rifle shot ended Earl Rule's life and he fell in the doorway.

Terrin was still tied to the hitching rail and couldn't do anything but watch helplessly. Cory Rule ran to the doorway and saw his pa and Rupert lying on the ground. He peered around the doorway and saw two Comanches riding towards the front of the house where Terrin was tied up.

In a panic, Cory rushed out the back door of the house to where they had left their horses. He didn't bother to saddle his horse, but merely grabbed the halter rope and snapped it onto the halter ring. Wasting no time he swung up on the horse bareback and kicked it into a full gallop.

There were two other Comanche warriors riding around to the back of the house and saw Cory riding away. Shots rang out from inside the house as Sam Pullman and the two hired hands armed themselves and began firing at the Comanches in front of the house.

One of the two Comanches that had seen Cory kicked his horse up and gave chase to the fleeing man. The other warrior went to the aid of the other members of the small war party who were in front of the house.

More shots rang out, but not from the Comanches or the ones inside the house. They came from a man on horseback who was barreling down the road that led to the Pullman house. It was Brian Sackett.

Brian killed two of the three remaining Comanche warriors causing the third member to high tail it out of there. Brian let him go. His concern was for the wellbeing of Terrin.

Brian hit the ground running as he approached the hitching rail where Terrin was still tied. He quickly cut the ropes loose that had her bound and covered her back with the torn remnant of her dress. He helped her into the house where her sister quickly attended to her.

Terrin wasn't hurt, just in a slight state of shock at what she had just gone through and what she had witnessed. Brian's concern for her was evident and impressed Terrin's sister.

"I think she'll be all right, Mr. Sackett. She's just a little shaken right now. You sure came along at the right time. Are the Rule's dead?" Eileen asked.

"Yeah, I'm pretty sure they are. I'll go out and check to make sure. You're sure you're okay, Terrin?" Brian asked concernedly.

"I'm all right, Brent don't worry. The whip never even touched me," Terrin said.

"The *whip* did you say? Do you mean they were going to whip you?" Brian said with a deep frown.

"She talked back to Mr. Rule and he was going to let the one named Rupert whip her. Terrin was able to stick a fork in his stomach though. Of course that didn't set well with the Rules," Eileen explained.

"I guess I did arrive at the right time. I'll be back in a minute. I'll check on the ones outside," Brian said as he started for the door.

When Brian got outside Sam Pullman and the two hired hands had just finished checking Rupert and Earl Rule's bodies.

"They're both dead, as well as the Indians. I'm sure glad you came along when you did, Sackett. Things were getting a little out of hand," Sam Pullman said.

"Yeah, you really know how to throw a 'welcome back' party," Brian said, getting a laugh from the three men.

Raymond D. Mason

Chapter 11

Lordsburg, New Mexico
Judd Vengeance's ranch house

Judd Vengeance sopped up the remnants of his dinner with a piece of bread and looked up at the man seated across from him. The man was Jack Yancey. Judd held his gaze for a moment and then spoke.

"So why should I put you up here until the heat dies down, Jack?" he asked.

"You owe me, Judd. I've done a couple of jobs for you that no one else was willing to do, remember? Besides, no one is going to come looking for me here in Vengeance Valley," Jack replied.

"Yeah, I'll have to give you that. You did do me a turn or two. Okay, you can hang your hat in the bunk house until the heat dies down. But, let me warn you, Jack; no rough stuff with my boys. I've got big plans and I'll need all the guns I can get to pull it off. The first time you stir up trouble with anyone, you're out of here. Do you hear me?" Vengeance stated.

"Hey, I'll be as meek as a kitten. I'm tired of running and hiding and eatin' cold food. I'll welcome your hospitality with open arms, believe me," Jack grinned.

"You know the procedure...breakfast at five thirty; supper at six. If you miss one you'll have to wait until the next meal to get anything out of the kitchen. Unless, that is you slip Cookie a little spending money. Just don't let me find out about it," Judd said.

"You're all heart, Judd," Yancey said.

"Go over and get yourself situated in the bunkhouse. Oh, and don't try and take one of the boys bunks who's already settled in. There's one empty bunk over there; that's the one you'll get," Judd ordered.

"Gotcha," Yancey said and downed the remainder of his coffee and got up.

He walked to the dining room door and looked back. "How's Towanda?"

"You just never mind her, Jack," Judd said. "She's still not over your last visit here. I don't think she likes you very much."

"Oh, she's crazy about me, Judd. She just puts on a front when other folks are around," Yancey grinned.

"Stay away from her. I mean it," Judd said with finality in his tone.

"Okay, okay. I was just wondering how she was, that's all," Yancey said and then laughed as he went on out of the room.

Yancey was about halfway to the bunkhouse when Towanda Lopez looked out her bedroom window. Towanda was the live in maid that also served as Judd's mistress when his wife was away.

"Oh no, not that animal again," she said in perfect English.

Hurriedly Towanda went downstairs in search of Judd Vengeance. When she finally found him she said angrily, "Judd, I told you I wouldn't stay in this house if that man was ever allowed back in."

"He'll only be here for a few days, Towanda. I need him to do a job for me and once he's done it, he'll be gone. He won't bother you this time, I promise," Judd said.

"He'd better not even look at me wrong, or I'll pack my things and go."

Judd bristled, "Where will you go, Towanda? Back to that sporting house I found you in? Is that where you want to go?"

"It would beat being in the same house with that animal. At least I'll have a little protection there," Towanda argued.

"Just simmer down. He's on the run and knows that if he leaves the valley he'd be caught and hanged within two days. He'll be aces while he's here. Mark my words," Judd stated.

Towanda cooled slightly in her tone of voice, "Well, okay...but remember what I said. That man is crazy and there's no telling what he might do."

"I'll keep a tight rein on him. If he gives you any trouble let me know," Judd stated.

A commotion outside caused them both to look towards the window.

"What's going on out there," Judd wondered aloud.

He walked over to the window and peered out. Yancey and one of the men who worked for Vengeance had squared off and had struck a gunfighter's pose.

"Oh, hell...he's already starting trouble," Judd said and rushed towards the door.

"I told you the man is nuts," Towanda said with a frown and shake of the head.

Judd ran outside just as Yancey pulled his gun and cocked the hammer back. Before Judd could say anything Yancey pulled the trigger and shot the man he'd been arguing with in the head. The mortally wounded man fell to the ground and went into a sort of spasm as he flopped around on the ground like a beheaded chicken.

Vengeance yelled out at the crazed gunman, "Yancey what have you done?"

"This guy started it, Judd. He called me a name and I don't let any body call me names, you know that," Yancey replied.

"What did he call you that would warrant shooting him?" Judd demanded.

"A kill crazy animal," Yancey said looking down at the dead man.

"I'd say you confirmed his reference, wouldn't you?" Judd answered.

"Who was this guy, anyone important to you?"

"No, actually he was just a hired hand who did odd jobs around the place," Judd said as he knelt down to check the man's head wound.

"It wasn't no big loss then, was it?" Yancey said as he removed the spent cartridge from the pistol's cylinder.

Guns of Vengeance Valley

When Judd rolled the dead man's body over and saw what the bullet had done to the back of the man's head he turned his face away quickly.

"My god, Yancey; this man didn't deserve this," Judd said.

"What time is supper, Judd?" Yancey asked as he looked back towards the house.

Judd looked at the man he'd just given permission to stay in the valley where he'd be safe from a posse. He couldn't have Yancey going crazy and killing his hired hands, but how would he get rid of him short of having the man shot?

Judd knew that Yancey would do things for him that none of the other men would do. He'd be valuable when it came to silencing a couple of people in Lordsburg, whether they were men or women. Yancey didn't seem to have a conscience when it came to killing people. He seemed to enjoy it. Still, if he got too bad he'd have to be killed; and Vengeance would be the one to do it.

Several of Judd's working cowboys rode into the yard and reined up when they saw the man lying on the ground with Judd and Yancey standing over him. After a couple of seconds they rode over to the dead body.

"What happened here, Judd?" one of the men asked.

Judd looked at the man then cast a quick glance at Yancey before returning his gaze towards the two hired hands.

"He thought he could take Yancey here on, but found out too late that he couldn't," Judd lied.

"Yancey? You don't mean this is Jack Yancey, do you Judd?" the man asked.

"Yeah, I'm Jack Yancey; does that bother you?"

Judd glared at the man as he said tightly, "Jack! Back off!"

"I didn't mean anything by my question, I was just going to say that I'd heard a lot about you lately," the man said with a half smile.

"Oh...what did you hear?" Yancey asked.

"I heard you were the lone gunman who robbed the Tucson stagecoach a couple of weeks ago. Killed a guard and two passengers, is that right?"

"Yeah, they didn't give me any choice," Yancey said giving Judd a quick glance.

"Nice to make your acquaintance," the man replied.

"Me too, the other hired hand said.

Yancey didn't reply, just merely nodded his head and grinned. He looked at himself as a celebrity of sorts. Once people got to know him, however, and saw how unstable he was their impression of him changed considerably.

"Would you boys mind taking care of Haney here?" Judd said motioning towards the dead man.

"Sure thing, Judd," one of the men said.

"Come on Jack, I'll show you the bunk I want you to take. And don't go arguing with anyone because you want to change bunks with them," Judd said with a perturbed look on his face.

He walked out to the bunkhouse with his growingly unwanted guest and showed him the bunk that was open. He warned him again about fighting with the other men before turning to go back to the house.

"You never did tell me when supper is," Yancey said.

Guns of Vengeance Valley

"Six o'clock, and don't be late," Judd said as he exited the bunkhouse.

Raymond D. Mason

Chapter 12

Brent Sackett tied up at the hitching rail in front of Brenda's Kitchen café. He had ridden into town to see if he could locate the man that Brenda had said was named Linc Sackett. While he was here he figured he would have a bite to eat.

Pushing the door open Brent entered the now crowded café due to it being so close to noon. He spotted an empty chair at a table occupied by three men who appeared to be working cowhands.

Walking up to the table he asked, "Mind if I join you men?"

One of the men looked up at him and frowned as he said, "Yeah, I mind."

Brent stood there for a moment and stared hard at the man. After a couple of seconds he pulled the chair out, threw his leg over the back of it and sat down.

"Maybe you didn't hear what I said?" the man snapped.

"And maybe I did. This is the only seat in the place and I'm hungry. You can go on with your conversation as if I wasn't here," Brent said.

Raymond D. Mason

The man looked around and spotted one other empty chair at a table that held the sheriff and two of his deputies.

"There's another empty space right over there with the sheriff. Move over there," the man groused.

"I don't like eating with lawmen. I'd rather eat with cowhands...even if one of them happens to be you," Brent said.

The man attempted to stare down Brent, but couldn't pull it off. Brent's stare soon withered the cowboy's resolve. Just as it did, Brenda passed by the table with an armload of plates on a serving tray.

"Hello Ma'am," Brent said when she stopped at the table next to the one where he was now seated.

"Oh, hello, how'd you sneak in without me seeing you?" she asked with a smile.

"It wasn't too difficult. Looks like you've got a booming business here," Brent replied.

"It's this way everyday around this time," Brenda said as she placed the plates in front of the men whose order she was delivering.

Brenda had a young woman working for her who was also busy delivering orders. Once Brenda had finished serving the table next to Brent's she turned and looked at him.

"What can I get for you? Brenda asked.

"I'll have what you just served there," Brent said motioning towards the table she'd just served.

"Ham and three eggs, two biscuits with honey, and hot coffee it is then," Brenda smiled.

"Make it four eggs and three biscuits," Brent said.

"Four and three it is. How do you want them?"

Guns of Vengeance Valley

"Fried," Brent said, getting a laugh from the men at his table along with Brenda. He then added quickly, "Over easy."

Brenda's smile lit widened. She was a pretty woman and her smile enhanced her good looks. Although Brent had not gotten over losing Julia he still appreciated Brenda's personality and attractiveness.

Two of the cowboys at the table Brent had joined warmed up towards him, but the one he'd had words with was still sullied up. Brent cast a quick glance at the man and noticed the furrowed brow.

"Lighten up, cowboy. Once I've had my breakfast you won't see me again," Brent offered.

"I don't like you," the man stated flatly.

"I don't care. Just don't let your dislike carry you to a place that puts you in harm's way and you'll be all right," Brent said evenly.

"Do you always come off so tough?" the man pressed.

"Drop it, Fred," one of the other men said.

"I won't drop it. This guy just makes himself right at home when I told him I didn't want him sitting here, so why should I drop it?" the man went on.

"It you value your health, you'll take your friend's advice," Brent said a slight frown forming.

"For two cents I'd take you outside and teach you a lesson," the man stated.

Brent didn't say a word as he reached in his pocket and pulled out quarter and tossed it on the table.

"I don't have two cents, but this will more than cover it," Brent said.

The cowboy looked at the coin and then at his two friends. He had worked himself into a corner and now it was time to put up or shut up. He decided to put up.

"I'll wait until you've had your meal and then we'll tussle," the man stated.

"It won't take long. Let's go. I'll be back before my breakfast is served," Brent said, getting a quick look from the man's two friends.

"It looks like your mouth has put your rear end in a sling, Fred," one of the men said getting a head nod from the other man.

Brent stood up and stared down at the man named Fred. Fred slowly got up from his chair and gave his two friends another quick glance.

"Lead the way," he said.

Brent turned and walked to the door. When he reached it Brenda called out to him.

"You're not leaving are you?" she asked.

"Nope, I just have to take care of something. I'll be back in a minute," Brent replied.

No sooner had they reached the boardwalk in front of the café than Fred leaped on Brent from the back, getting him in a headlock.

Brent pushed Fred away and before anyone knew what had happened, hit the man with three sharp jabs to the face. Blood began to run from Fred's nose. The blows brought tears to his eyes and he never saw the hard right hand that landed flush on his jaw.

Fred dropped straight down to his knees. Before he could gather himself, a short right hand clipped him on the chin, snapping his head back and rendering him unconscious.

Brent rubbed his knuckles and looked at Fred's friends.

"Tell him he can keep the quarter," Brent said as he walked back inside the café with everyone staring at him.

Brent sat down and looked around the room at the gawkers. From behind him a man's voice said, "Yep, he's got to be a Sackett."

Brent looked around quickly and saw two men standing behind his chair. They were both wearing grins and moved around and took a seat at the table.

"You must be Brent Sackett?" the man who'd spoke earlier reiterated.

"And you are?" Brent asked.

"Lincoln Sackett," Linc grinned as he held out his hand.

"The lady that owns the café said that you were in town," Brent said as he shook Linc's hand. "How've you been?"

"Okay...and you?" Linc replied.

The two looked at one another for a moment not knowing what to say next. Finally Linc said, "Oh, this is my friend, Clay Butler."

"How do you do, Clay?" Brent said and shook Clay's hand.

"So, you're heading for California, huh?" Linc said.

When Brent took on a questioning look Linc stated, "Brenda, the owner here, told me."

"Oh, yeah...so what do you do, Linc?" Brent asked.

"We're business partners," Linc said motioning towards Clay. "Rodeo stock," Linc said proudly.

"Oh, really...you must have quite a stable?" Brent said showing his interest.

"Right now we've only got one horse, but he's a buck jumper like you ain't ever seen before," Linc stated and looked at Clay who gave an agreeing nod.

"He must be. So does he make you much money?" Brent pressed.

"He's going to, you can bet on it," Brent grinned.

"One horse," Brent pondered.

Just then Brenda brought Brent's order which cut the conversation short. The two cousins just couldn't think of a lot to say to one another. Linc and Clay took the opportunity to place their orders with Brenda further allowing them to cut short their conversation with Brent.

Once Brenda had taken Linc and Clay's order Brent opened up a little more.

"Let's see, you're my uncle Dave and Patty's son, ain't that right?"

"Yeah, well, they raised me from the time I was two years old and gave me the Sackett name. I don't even remember my real ma and pa. I look at them as my real folks," Linc said.

"Where are you from, Butler?" Brent asked.

"Cottonwood...well, just out of there a ways."

"I see. What brings you two to Lordsburg?" Brent asked.

"He got fired from a ranch and I quit," Clay said quickly.

Brent looked at Linc for a moment and said, "That sounds like a Sackett."

The three of them broke into laughter and their conversation became a lot less strained.

"So what was the little discussion you were having with the man outside all about?" Linc asked.

"He didn't want me sitting at their table and the only other seat available was the one with the sheriff and his deputies over there," Brent said with a head nod in the lawmen's direction.

Linc and Butler looked that way and Linc grinned, "I take it you don't like lawmen?"

"It ain't that so much. I was one for a spell. I just don't like to eat with them. They'll steal the food right off your plate," Brent joked.

"That's good enough for me," Linc said with another chuckle.

"Me too," Clay agreed.

Once they had finished their meals they said goodbye and Brent headed back to meet up with the others traveling with him. Linc and Clay went and checked on their bucking bronco and made sure he was well fed.

While they were at the livery stable two cowboys rode up and one had a flier in his hand. They called out to the stable owner if he could tell them where the ones with the bucking bronco were.

"They just happen to be right here," the owner said and pointed towards Linc and Clay.

The cowboys dismounted and walked over to where the two 'rodeo men' were standing. Linc looked in their direction as they approached.

"Howdy, are you the ones with the bronc you say no one can ride?" the shorter of the two asked.

"That's us, and that's the horse," Linc grinned.

"I've got five that says I can ride it," the short one said.

"Let's see it," Linc said and pulled fifty dollars out of his pocket.

They saddled the horse and led it out to the corral. The horse stood perfectly still while the cowboy cautiously climbed aboard. Once situated atop the horse, he said, "Let her rip."

Linc stepped back from the horse and it turned and looked at him for a second and then leaped sideways a good six feet. The move was all it took for the cowboy to go flying off, having expected the horse to go upwards.

The next cowboy in line laughed, "I guess that fifty belongs to me."

He took his turn on the bronc and lasted three jumps before winding up on the seat of his britches. Once the horse got rid of its rider, it stopped bucking. The two cowboys stood staring at the big horse and merely shook their heads in amazement.

"You men have got you a real money maker there," one of the cowhands said.

"We think so," Clay said. "Why, we'll make money we ain't even spent yet."

The two cowboys looked at Clay as he and Linc began laughing. This was their first customers, but there would be more to come. Here it was not even ten o'clock in the morning and the horse had already made them ten bucks.

Chapter 13

Tucson, Arizona

Bob and Shelah Colton had just climbed aboard the stagecoach for the next leg of their trip to California. Their traveling companions were a man and woman on their way to Yuma and a man who said he was a lawyer.

"So where are you folks headed?" the lawyer said as he eyed the beautiful Shelah Colton.

"Out to the Monterey, California area," Bob replied.

"Beautiful country out there," the lawyer said casting a quick glance at Bob before returning his attention to Shelah.

"Oh, you've been there, have you?" Bob questioned.

"Several times; I travel from my home in San Diego up to San Francisco several times a year. Like I said, beautiful country up that way," Vengeance answered.

"Where are you headed now?" Bob asked.

"I'm on my way to San Diego. That's where my practice is. I've been to Lordsburg to see my brother and give him some legal advice. My name is John

Vengeance," he said extending his hand towards Bob.

The other man in the coach gave his wife a quick look when he heard the name John Vengeance. His wife returned the look and then they turned their attention back towards the others in the coach.

Vengeance shook hands with Colton and then looked towards the other couple onboard the coach, eyeing the woman first and then the man. It was obvious John Vengeance had an eye for the ladies and didn't care if the husband was present or not.

After checking the other couple out thoroughly, Vengeance looked back at Colton and said, "I don't believe I caught your name?"

"No you didn't. That's because I didn't give it," Bob replied and then added with a slight grin, "Colton, Bob Colton."

"And you are?" Vengeance said giving Shelah a charming smile.

"His wife," Shelah stated returning her own smile.

"Oh...I see," Vengeance said and then turned his attention towards the other couple.

"And you folks are heading where?" Vengeance asked.

"We're just going to Yuma. My wife's sister is quite ill and we're going to take care of her until she gets back on her feet," the man stated with a steady gaze at Vengeance.

"I guess you heard my name, John Vengeance; what might your names' be?" Vengeance asked.

The man's face tightened when he heard the name of the man seated directly across from him for the second time. The man's wife gave her husband a quick look and put her hand on his arm before returning her attention towards Vengeance.

"Since your name is Vengeance and you just came from Lordsburg you must be related to Judd Vengeance, am I right?" the man asked.

"He's my brother. Why? Do you know him?" Vengeance asked with a smile.

The man's face slowly took on an angry, tortured look, "Oh, yeah. I know your brother. He's a no good, low down dirty skunk and nothing more than a desperado with the law on his side. A law that's bought and paid for by him, I might add," the man said, his words and anger filling the coach with tension.

Bob Colton wanted to hear more on this and asked, "I take it you know this man's brother?"

"Oh, yeah, I know him alright. He stole our homestead from us. He wanted the water we had and pulled some legal shenanigans to get it. I don't like your brother and if you gave him legal advice on his dirty deeds...then I don't like you either," the man snapped.

John Vengeance held a hard, steady gaze on the man, but didn't respond immediately. After several long, thought filled seconds he replied.

"You homesteaders are all alike. You take root on another man's property and when he wants you to move on, you cry like a bunch of spoiled kids. I gave my brother legal advice because dozens of your kinds were moving in on his range land and squatting like a bunch of nesting hens.

"You think men like my brother just claimed that land and didn't have to fight for it? He fought the ones who held Spanish land grants; and then he fought the Apaches. He had to deal with droughts, and floods, cyclones and dust storms.

"He buried his wife and one of our brothers. He lost good hard working cowhands to rustlers and braved thousand mile cattle drives to keep from losing everything he'd worked so hard to build up.

"Yes, he has pulled some legal 'shenanigans' as you call them, but it was in order to expand the West. He's responsible for bringing civilization to that area and your kind wants to take it all away from him.

"Where were you when the Apaches attacked his ranch and killed seven of his cowhands? Where were you when his wife got sick with the fever and lingered for over a month, dying a little bit more each day?

"Why didn't you give him a hand when Buffalo Horn and fifty of his braves attacked the herd and ran three hundred head of cattle off a steep ravine, killing them all?

"No, you just want to come along after all the dirty work has been done and stake a claim and live in peace and harmony. Well it doesn't work that way. Sure, my brother is ruthless, but he had to be to survive in this godforsaken country.

"How much sand do you have, mister? Enough to take one half of what my brother had to do in order to carve his empire out of this hot, hard land. I doubt it seriously.

"You go ahead and hate him and me all you want to, but remember this. It took blood, sweat, and tears to make it out here. You've only shed the sweat and maybe a few tears. Wait until the blood starts to

Guns of Vengeance Valley

flow and then let's see how you stand up," John Vengeance said.

Bob Colton looked at Shelah who gave him a quick look. They'd heard of Judd Vengeance and that he was a ruthless man, but also a very wealthy one. Colton not only knew of Judd Vengeance but had sworn to get even with him for something involving one of Colton's friends.

Suddenly Bob Colton had an idea. He just might be able to work this chance meeting into a profit. He'd have to gather his thoughts and run them by Shelah. She was great at coming up with workable suggestions.

The man seated across from Vengeance didn't respond to what the attorney had said to him, not right away. He pondered the words for a moment and finally spoke his mind.

"You forgot one thing about your brother, Mr. Vengeance. He has hired guns working for him whose main job it is to see that anyone who gets in his way is dealt with quickly and severely. In my world they call it 'murder'. What do they call it in yours?"

"Judd has some men who are there to protect his ranch against marauders, that's true. If they do things on their own, that's not my brother's concern. If a man is on the run from the law, he's not welcome on my brother's ranch," John said, believing his own words.

"Are you aware of the fact that Billy the Kid, John Wesley Hardin, and for a span of about three weeks, Dirty Dave Rudabaugh, have worked for your brother? Those men are nothing more than man-killers," the man stated.

Vengeance didn't respond. He had not known this bit of information. He didn't know if it was true or just a claim made by this man.

"I suppose you have proof of this? After all, anyone can make a claim about something that has absolutely no validity to it," Vengeance said.

"The next time you're in Lordsburg stop by the sheriff's office and ask him. He'll tell you exactly what I just did. Everyone in Lordsburg knows your brother and what he's about," the man said.

That was what Bob Colton was looking for, the final piece to his idea. If Judd Vengeance was planning something that would require hired guns, it had to be something very big. Colton knew a number of good gun hands that would jump at the chance to use their guns in a range war; if the price was right.

Just then the man riding shotgun climbed atop the stagecoach while the driver looked in the passenger's window and said, "We're heading out for Yuma now, folks. I'll try to give you as comfortable ride as possible. You might want to pull the shade down if the dust coming inside gets too bad."

Bob Colton opened the door, causing the driver to step back. He smiled as he said, "Come on Shelah, we're on the wrong stagecoach."

Shelah looked puzzled, but followed her husband as he-- disembarked. The driver gave them a look of dismay.

"We want to go to Lordsburg," Bob said with a smile.

"Didn't you just come from there?" the driver asked.

"Yeah, but we forgot something back there," Bob replied.

"Oh...what's that?" the driver asked.

"A whole bunch of money," Colton said with a wry grin.

Raymond D. Mason

Chapter
14

The Sackett Ranch
Abilene, Texas

Brian Sackett looked across the table at his father, John. John wore a very worried expression on his face as he stared into his coffee cup. Brian knew what was on his father's mind; poisoned waterholes.

Finally John looked up and said, "If we don't find out who's doing this, Brian, we could lose half our herd. If that happens...well, I don't know what we'll do. I want you and AJ to split up the ranch hands equally and find every water hole that's been affected by whoever...or whatever it is that's poisoning our water.

"Okay, Pa. AJ has four of the men out right now checking the waterholes to the north. I'll take four and head south," Brian said and then added. "How many head of cattle have we lost so far?"

"Roughly a thousand head, but we haven't checked all the waterholes yet. Get on it and find out what's causing this," John said firmly.

"Right away," Brian said and downed the remainder of his coffee, picked up his hat and headed out the door.

"Be careful, son. It could be Comanches."

"I will, Pa."

Brian headed out to the corral where a couple of ranch hands, Slim and Wiley, were training a couple of cutting horses. He called them over to him and explained that he wanted them to go with him to check on the waterholes to the south.

"Have you seen Chalky and Dauber Ray?" Brian asked.

"Yeah, they were cleaning out the stalls in the barn earlier. I guess they're still there," the man known as Slim said.

"I'll get them to go with us. You boys get ready to ride. I'll be right back," Brian said.

Brian left the two men and walked to the barn to get Chalky and Dauber Ray. The barn door was slightly ajar and as Brian started inside he heard the two men start laughing. He stopped short to see what it was they found so funny.

"Wait until the boys start the grass fire. That's really going to have the Sacketts in an uproar," the man named Chalky said.

"When is that supposed to happen?" Dauber Ray asked.

"Tonight is what I heard. With the cattle being near the box canyon they won't be able to get away from the fire and about 800 head will be barbecued," Chalky replied.

Brian's jaws tightened. These two were involved with the ones who had been poisoning the waterholes and now they were planning a grass fire.

Guns of Vengeance Valley

Brian knew what they were planning on doing, but he still didn't know where exactly.

Brian quickly thought about the various herds of cattle they had on the ranch and which herd could be in danger. The only herd that was near a box canyon was the one near a place called Puma Canyon. And there were at least 800 head of cattle up there.

He would have to work fast if they were going in order to save the herd. Thank God he had time to gather enough men to stop the intended burn out. He'd have to send a rider for AJ and the other men, though.

At first Brian thought about confronting the two men in the barn, but thought better of it. He could always get his hands on them. Besides, he didn't want to tip off the others involved in this scheme that he was on to them.

Brian went back out to where Slim and Wiley were waiting for him. He gave a quick look over his shoulder in the direction of the barn and then turned towards Slim.

"Slim, I want you to ride out to where AJ and the other men are and tell AJ I said to get back here as fast as they can. We'll be heading for Puma Canyon as soon as it gets dark. And Slim, hurry; it's important," Brian stated.

Slim left the horse he'd been training to cut and mounted his own mount. He kicked the horse into a full gallop. Brian then turned to Wiley, whom he knew he could trust.

"Wiley, I want you to do a favor for me," Brian said.

"Sure thing, boss, anything at all; what is it?" Wiley asked.

111

Raymond D. Mason

"I want you to keep an eye on Chalky and Dauber Ray. But, don't let them know you're watching them whatever you do," Brian said.

"Okay, that shouldn't be a problem. Am I supposed to be looking for anything in particular?"

"If they should leave the ranch, I want you to make a special note of which way they head and then come and get me. And come running," Brian stated emphatically.

"Is something afoot, Brian?" Wiley asked.

"I'll say. We stand to lose around 800 head of cattle tonight and I ain't about to let it happen. Now, remember; don't let them know they're being watched and let me know the minute they take off," Brian repeated.

"Are they still in the barn?"

"Yeah, that's where they're at now. I'm going to the house to talk to my pa, so act busy, but keep an eye out for Chalky and Dauber."

Brian headed back in the direction of the main house and Wiley took up a position where he wouldn't be noticed by the two men he was to keep an eye on.

It didn't come as any big surprise to Wiley that Brian was suspicious of the two he had him watching of doing something underhanded. He'd had a hunch about those two ever since they'd been hired three months earlier.

There was just something shifty about both men. For one thing they wouldn't come clean about the area from which they hailed. Most men are proud to tell you about their hometown or territory; but not these two.

Slim found AJ and the other ranch hands and relayed the message sent by Brian. AJ wasted no time in getting the men headed back to the ranch. If there was the slightest chance that they could find the ones responsible for the poisoned waterholes, AJ wanted to make them pay.

Once back at the ranch Brian filled AJ in on what all he'd heard from the two in the barn. AJ patted the pistol on his hip and said.

"We'll give those hombres a warm reception when they start to set that grass fire."

John Sackett had heard everything and added, "But make sure the ones carrying the torches don't drop them or they may succeed in burning up those cattle. The grass is as dry as it can be due to the drought-like conditions we've been having. If one of them should drop one of their torches it will spread like...well, like wild fire."

"Yeah, we'll have to be real careful," Brian replied.

"We'll take them before they ever fire the torches up," AJ offered.

"If we can catch them in the throat of the canyon it's mostly hardpan and rock. Of course, we'll have to let them get within ten yards of waterhole," Brian answered.

"Let's hope there're no more than three or four of them. The fewer the better of our chances of keeping 'em away from the dry grass and brush," AJ said thoughtfully.

"I could take some of the men and take up a position that would put them in crossfire. That way they'd have no possible way of escape," Brian said.

"I hope this doesn't put us in trouble with the law. That's all we'd need is for us to have to take it on the run too. I don't think Pa would like it too much having three sons on the dodge," AJ grinned.

Chapter 15

Brian and two of the Sackett wranglers took up a position behind some rocks a good forty inside the narrow entrance to Puma Canyon. AJ and four other men positioned themselves behind rocks about thirty feet above the canyon's entrance.

The men coming to poison the waterhole would be caught in crossfire and wouldn't stand a chance of getting to the waterhole about a hundred yards inside the canyon. Both Brian and AJ felt bad about laying a trap like this, but it had to be done.

While they waited for the arrival of whoever it was who had been poisoning the waterholes, they talked about what was about to happen.

AJ asked one of his men, a man named Kruger if he'd ever been in a shootout before.

"Yeah, I've been in a number of them, but that was different; it was during the War. I've never bushwhacked someone though. I don't feel real good about waylaying someone," Kruger stated.

"That's right, you were in the War, wasn't you, Kruger?" AJ asked.

"Yes, and I hated it. We were called on to do some pretty terrible things to fellas some of us knew. We did it because of what we stood for and they fought back for the same reason. It was a crazy mixed up War, but I guess it had to be fought to save the nation," Kruger said.

"Yeah, that's what both Brian and Brent have said, too. I didn't fight in the War because someone had to stay and help Pa on the ranch. My sympathies lay with the North, I guess. Of course, Brent's lay with the South as you probably know," AJ explained.

"I fought for the North like Brian did. It's amazing how we had to focus on the uniforms of the enemy and not on the men wearing them. It made it easier shooting at a uniform instead of the man wearing it. I still lost sleep over it though. You can only fool your conscience for so long, I guess," Kruger stated.

Meanwhile behind the rocks where Brian and his men were positioned, Brian was in a conversation with a man they called Nevada simply because he said he hailed from there.

"Are you scared, Brian?" Nevada asked.

"Yeah, I'm always scared when shooting starts. You never know which bullet might have your name on it. It would be so much better if we could have had a showdown with these hombres during the day. The night holds a little more terror than shooting it out in broad daylight," Brian replied.

"I don't mind telling you I'm scared. The only time I've been involved in a scrape where hot lead was being thrown around was when Black Jack Haggerty and his men came barreling down on the ranch last year," Nevada stated.

"That's right you had just been hired as I recall," Brian replied.

"Yeah, that was some 'getting acquainted' party your pa threw for me. I was about ready to hightail it back to Nevada," he chuckled.

Just then the sound of horses approaching caught their ears. Brian put his finger to his lips and cocked his head to one side in order to hear a little better.

He gave Nevada a glance and got an agreeing head nod from him. It was too dark to see AJ and the others, but they had to have heard the approaching horses as well.

AJ and his men sat in anticipation for what was about to happen. AJ squinted to see into the darkness in hopes of spotting the riders. Finally he did; there were four men.

As they drew near enough for AJ to make them out he recognized the lead rider as Jess Whittington, one of their neighboring ranchers. Jess and John Sackett had been one time friends, but Jess accused John of stealing yearlings and it brought their friendship to an abrupt end.

There had been no truth to the claim that the Sackett's were stealing the calves. In fact, the same men responsible for stealing Whittington's cattle were also stealing from John Sackett.

Whittington, however, had sworn to get even with John for what he imagined as a wrong committed against him. This might be his way of getting back at his one time friend.

AJ knew they would have to wait and make sure that the waterhole was the riders intended destination. It didn't take long to find it out. They reined their horses into the mouth of Puma Canyon and the waterhole was only located just beyond.

Brian waited until the men were about twenty yards from his position before calling out, "Hold it right there."

The moment Brian called out to the riders they went for their guns and shots were fired. As soon as AJ and his men heard the shots they opened fire on the four riders.

Being caught in crossfire, the riders didn't stand a chance. Although it was dark, Brian and AJ's shots found their mark and knocked men out of the saddle. The gunfight only lasted about thirty seconds. Once the last shot was fired the area became deathly silent.

Brian slowly moved out from his hiding place as did the others. AJ jumped down to the ground and they moved in to check on the riders that were lying motionless.

AJ called out to the Sackett riders, "Is everyone accounted for?"

"Everyone is okay here," Brian replied.

"Good, we're all right as well. Now let's see who our visitors are," AJ said.

Brian moved over to the nearest man on the ground to him and rolled him over so he could see his face. He didn't recognize the man at first, but did notice a pocket watch in the man's vest pocket. He pulled it out and checked the inscription on the back. It read Justin Whittington.

"AJ, this is one of Jess Whittington's sons," Brian called out.

"Which one is it?" AJ replied.

"Justin."

"He's the youngest one of the Whittington boys. This one over here is Harley, he's the middle boy," AJ called back.

"I know this jasper," Nevada said as he checked one of the dead men. "They called him Pancake Parker, because he could eat so many. I rode with him up in Wyoming six years back."

"Hey, AJ," Kruger said called out loudly. "I think this is Whittington's oldest son, Junior."

All four men were dead. Jess Whittington had lost all of his sons in this shootout. This wasn't going to end here, and both Brian and AJ knew it. The Whittington's had a lot of family scattered around Texas and they were a tight knit clan, to be sure.

"Round up their horses and then load 'em up," AJ said. "We'll take 'em back to the ranch and I'll take them over tomorrow so Jess can bury them. This is not going to sit well with him, I can tell you that."

Raymond D. Mason

Chapter 16

John Sackett shook his head as he stared down at the dead men Brian and AJ had brought back to the ranch. You could see the pain in his face as he slowly shook his head negatively.

"I was there when Justin was born. I never seen a man any more proud of a baby than Jess was at that very moment. This is going to break his heart," John said.

"I'll take the bodies over to his place in the buckboard, Pa," AJ said with a frown.

John looked at him quickly and said, "No, we'll all take the boys back to Jess. This is not going to be an easy thing for him to handle. There's no telling what he might do. No, we'll all go, AJ."

AJ cast a quick glance at Brian who looked sadly at the bodies lying on the ground. He and Junior Whittington were about the same age and the two had always fought with one another as kids. It wasn't that they hated each other it was just that they were both so competitive.

"Why'd they do it, Pa?" Brian asked. "Do you think Jess put them up to it?"

"I don't know, Brian. I hope not. I'd hate to think Jess would stoop to something that low, but who knows the heart of a man; no one but God Almighty," John replied.

"Do you think this could lead to an all out war between the Whittington's and us?" AJ asked.

"It could, what with the hard feelings Jess already holds towards me. We'll have to be ready just in case. I want two men riding the north range instead of just one from now on. At least until we know how Jess is going to take this," John said thoughtfully.

"We'd better get these bodies over to the Whittington ranch. They'll start to ripen before long," AJ commented drawing a slight frown from John.

AJ noticed and said quickly, "I didn't mean for that to come out that way. I'm sorry, Pa."

"I know, I know. You're right, though. Brian, I want you to go and get a couple of the boys to ride along with us. No sense in taking any chances Jess might go off and start a shooting feud," John stated.

Brian sent one of the ranch hands to hitch up the buckboard and bring it around to where the bodies were. They loaded them into the back of it and covered them with a tarp. Once they had done that they mounted up for the long ride over to the Whittington ranch.

Vengeance Valley
Lordsburg, New Mexico

"What do you mean there's some folks staying down in that grove of trees on the way into town?" Judd Vengeance snapped angrily.

Guns of Vengeance Valley

"Just that Mr. Vengeance; there's actually two wagons down there and we told 'em they were on Vengeance land and would have to leave," Ben Wallace stated.

"You know I don't like squatters nestin' on my range. Give 'em an inch and they'll take a mile. Why didn't you run 'em off, Ben," Vengeance asked, glaring at Wallace.

"I was going to, but Joel Holbrook said he'd been in the War with one of the men. A man by the name of Brent Sackett," Holbrook answered.

"Sackett...I've met the man. He's a hard case from what I could tell. Keep an eye on them and if it looks like they're going to stay awhile," Vengeance said and then had another thought.

A smile came to his face and then a slight chuckle, "Go over to the bunk house and tell Yancey I want to see him. I've got a little job for him to do."

Holbrook took on a troubled look as he said, "Is Jack Yancey here?"

"Yeah, why...you know him, Ben, don't you?"

"Oh yeah I know him all right. All the ranch hands either know him or know of him. That man is crazy as an Apache on peyote. If you even look at him wrong you're in danger of being either shot or knifed," Wallace said seriously.

"Just tell him I want to see him, he won't give you any trouble," Judd said and thought of how Yancey would handle the situation.

Wallace left the main house and walked across the barnyard to the bunkhouse. He opened the door and peered inside. Yancey was lying on his bunk holding a cigarette between his fingers, but was sound asleep. Wallace almost tiptoed across the room and when he was standing by Yancey's bunk looked down at the lit cigarette.

The cigarette had burned down to a point that the fired ash was between the fingers holding the smoke, but Yancey was dead to the world; sound asleep.

"How can he sleep with the cigarette burning between his fingers like that?" Wallace said to himself.

About that time Yancey rolled over and dropped the cigarette onto the floor. Wallace stepped on it, crushing it out. When he looked at Yancey's fingers he saw why the hot end of the cigarette hadn't hurt him. His fingers were one big scar from just that; hot cigarette burns.

Wallace backed up a few paces and cleared his throat loudly. The sleeping Yancey didn't move which forced Wallace to reach over and touch him on the shoulder. He'd no sooner pulled his hand away than Yancey sat straight up, whipped out his pistol and aimed it straight at Wallace's head.

Wallace froze. Yancey's eyes were as wide as those of the startled Wallace. The two men stood staring into each others eyes until finally Yancey blinked several times and seemed to relax somewhat.

He took a deep breath and muttered, "What is it?"

Mr. Vengeance wants to see you up at the house. I think he has a job he wants you to do," Wallace said breathing easier.

Yancey nodded his head slowly and then said, "Don't ever touch me when I'm sleeping. You're lucky you're still alive."

"Don't worry, Yancey. I won't," Wallace said and moved away slowly.

Yancey got up and slipped his boots on before grabbing his hat and walking out of the bunkhouse. When he got to what the ranch hands called 'the big house' he didn't bother to knock, but just went on inside.

Judd Vengeance and Towanda the live in maid were in a somewhat compromising position, but Yancey's intrusion abruptly halted their passionate embrace.

"Well, well, well," Yancey said with a grin. "Look what I found."

"You could knock once in awhile, Jack," Vengeance snapped.

"I wouldn't have to unless you had something to hide," Yancey said still grinning.

"Come in the other room. I have something I want you to take care of. And I want the job done tonight," Vengeance stated.

Towanda glared at Yancey as she turned and started up the stairs to her room. Yancey tipped his hat to her and laughed as he followed Vengeance into the other room.

Once inside, Yancey asked, "What is it you want me to do...or should I say, who is it you want me to kill? That is it, isn't it Judd?"

"I want some nesters moved off my land. I'll tell you where they are and you go down there and make sure they're gone come morning," Vengeance said as he grabbed a piece of paper and a pencil and began sketching a map for Yancey to follow.

"How many of them are there?" Yancey asked.

"Two wagon loads," Judd replied.

"No problem. Is this something that I get paid for, or is this one on the house?"

Vengeance thought for a moment and then said, "I'll give you a hundred dollars if you kill one of them. His name is Sackett, Brent Sackett."

"Looks like I'm going to be a hundred dollars richer come morning," Yancey grinned.

"He might not be too easy to bring down, Jack. I've heard a few tales about him from one of my ranch hands."

"Tales; tales ain't nothing but talk. Until you've seen it for yourself, Judd, you can't believe anything you've heard tell about someone or something; and you ain't seen this guy do a thing, am I right?" Yancey replied.

"No, I guess not. But you do have to consider the source. If it's from a reliable person you can put some credence in it," Vengeance argued.

"Whatever. Don't worry, like I said, they'll be gone come morning," Yancey said pulling his pistol and spinning the cylinder.

The Whittington Ranch
Near Abilene, Texas

Jess Whittington pulled the canvas back and peered at the bodies of his sons. He lowered his head and groaned making a low, guttural sound. When he looked up he had tears in his eyes. Whittington turned and looked at John Sackett and said sadly, "Why John? Why did this happen?"

"I'm sorry Jess, I am truly sorry. Someone has been poisoning our water and we had to find out who it was, that's why it happened. If I'd had any idea it was your sons doing it I'd have come to you first. We had no way of knowing though," John explained.

"What reason could my boys have for poisoning your waterholes John, tell me that?" Jess asked, his hurt holding back his anger.

"If I knew, Jess, I would tell you. I thought maybe you could tell me why?"

"Are you saying they did it because I put them up to it?" Jess asked with a deep set frown.

"I'm not saying that, Jess. I'm just saying that something prompted them to do it. Maybe they misunderstood something you said," John said sympathetically.

"You're saying I put them up to it, aren't you?"

"No, I'm not saying that at all, Jess."

Whittington grew silent for a moment and then straightened to his full height.

"You know that this means war, don't you John? I'm not about to let these murders go unpunished. You will pay and you will pay dearly," Whittington said in a low growl.

"Jess, a feud ain't going to settle anything. We didn't do this on purpose. We were just protecting what is ours. Like I said, if I'd had any way of knowing that your sons were...," John said but was cut off.

"I know what you said, but I'm telling you this right now. You will pay for every drop of blood my boys shed when you gunned 'em down. Now I suggest you get off my ranch while you still can. The next time we meet you had better be wearing your gun, John Sackett," Whittington said with a snarl in his voice.

John took a deep breath and shook his head. He cast a quick glance at Jess and then turned to Brian and AJ and said, "Come on boys, we've done all we can do here."

Whittington stood with his fists clenched as he watched John, Brian, and AJ walk away. This feud had just taken a deadly turn and it could only mean more deaths as far as Jess Whittington was concerned.

The Sackett's rode home in silence. Each one felt bad about what had happened, but there was nothing they could do about it now. The die had been cast and from here on they'd have to keep their eyes wide open for ambushes by Jesse Whittington's clan, and his riders.

Chapter 17

Lordsburg, NM
10 pm

The stagecoach from Tucson pulled into the Wells Fargo depot and the driver called out the stop.

"Lordsburg, folks; everybody out," he yelled out.

The first ones off the stage were Bob and Shelah Colton. They took their bags from the driver and walked down the street in the direction of the Lordsburg Hotel. They would go out to see Judd Vengeance the next morning.

Bob Colton had an idea he wanted to run by Vengeance and if the rancher went for it, would mean a hefty sum for Bob and Shelah. It had to do with some property near this new town called Tombstone and a mine he'd heard about that was being dug.

There was no mine, however, not really. Colton knew of an old mine that had not panned out and had been abandoned. If he could get Vengeance to go for the deal he would go back and salt the mine to make it look like Vengeance was getting something

Raymond D. Mason

for next to nothing. In truth, the one getting something for nothing would be him and Shelah.

Bob Colton had heard of Judd Vengeance due to a friend of his being gunned down by one of Vengeance's hired guns. Colton had sworn that one day he would get even with the rancher for killing his friend. If he could do it by getting into Vengeance's pocket book, that would be even sweeter.

After checking into the hotel Bob and Shelah headed for one of the nicer gambling halls in town. They wanted to play some poker and Shelah was as good at the game as was Bob. They had no trouble finding a game where both could sit in.

Between the two of them they managed to walk away with over three hundred dollars in winnings. After sharing a bottle of champagne they went back to the hotel room and straight to bed. It had been a long day and they were both dead tired.

It was around midnight when something awakened Brent Sackett. He lay under the wagon and listened intently to the sounds of the night. He slowly reached over and pulled his pistol from its holster. He'd heard whispers and they weren't coming from the wagons, but rather from behind some brush.

Brent cocked the hammer on his Colt back very slowly so it would not make that distinct sound that only a gun being cocked makes. He watched the underbrush and finally saw movement.

When he saw leather boots through the underbrush he knew it wasn't Apaches. No, they belonged to either white men or Mexicans. He took

Guns of Vengeance Valley

aim at the open space the men would have to pass through in order to get into their camp.

When the first man appeared in the opening he held a rifle in his hands and was attempting to walk very softly. Brent leveled his pistol at the man and waited to see how many more were out there.

He quickly determined that there were only three men invading their camp and they all had their guns drawn. It was only then that he opened fire on the intruders.

The first man that was hit was Ben Wallace. The bullet from Brent's gun hit him in the shoulder of his gun hand. He let out a cry of pain that coupled with the gunshot woke up the others in the wagons. Brent fired again and that shot too brought a scream of pain.

The third man was Jack Yancey and he fired several shots towards the wagons, but made a hasty retreat back in the direction of their horses. Brent scrambled out from under the wagon and gave chase, but it was too dark for him to see the man escaping.

Brent checked the men he'd shot and recognized Ben Wallace right away as having been one of the men who visited their campsite the day before. The second man Brent had shot was dead.

Brent knelt down and checked the wound to Wallace's shoulder. It was a bad wound and the bullet had not passed through. He would need to be operated on to remove the slug.

"What were you attacking us for?" Brent asked.

"Judd Vengeance wants you out of here. You're on his range and he fears you are squatters," Wallace stated truthfully.

"We're not squatters. Who was the man who got away?" Brent demanded.

Wallace thought about the question and pondered whether he should tell Sackett who it was. Finally he figured it would be better for everyone if Sackett knew.

"Jack Yancey," Wallace said.

Just then Mrs. Keeling called out, "Brent, it's Mr. Dobbs. I think he's dead."

Brent made sure there were no guns within Wallace's reach before rushing to the wagon that Dobbs had been sleeping under. He crawled under the wagon and rolled Dobbs over. Sure enough, he was dead with a bullet hole in his head.

Brent closed his eyes and lowered his head for a second and then thought about the children. He quickly crawled out from under the wagon and called to Mrs. Keeling.

"Are the children all right? Grant, are you okay?" he then called out.

"Yeah, Brent, I'm okay and so is the baby," Grant called back.

Brent breathed a sigh of relief and looked back in Wallace's direction. He walked back to the wounded Wallace and continued to question him.

"So this Jack Yancey fella was with you, huh? I take it he headed back to Vengeance's ranch," Brent said with a deep frown.

"Yeah, the man is crazy. He let us take the lead so if anyone got shot it would be us. He's supposed to be so tough, but if you ask me he's one of the biggest cowards I've ever seen," Wallace snapped.

"You'll have to see a doctor and have that slug removed. I'll see to it you get into town. Just let me

Guns of Vengeance Valley

get the horse hooked up to one of the wagons," Brent said.

"Why are you so concerned about my well being? We had come to run you out of here."

"To be honest, I don't know why. Perhaps it's because you were just doing your job, or I don't know? Maybe you weren't planning on killing us? Were you?" Brent asked directly.

"No, I didn't want to kill you. I'll tell you one thing though. Yancey would have killed you in a heart beat," Wallace said truthfully.

"I'll take care of this Yancey character. You say he probably headed back to Vengeance's ranch house?"

"Yeah, but if I was you, Sackett, I wouldn't go there. That is an armed camp. He's got hired guns coming in there every couple of days. He's got some big plans for something. I think it might be a huge land grab. Whatever it is he feels he needs a lot of firepower," Wallace confided seeing as how he was being treated by Brent Sackett.

Raymond D. Mason

Chapter 18

"I'll go with you Brent," Grant Holt said once the two had hitched up one of the teams to Dobbs's wagon.

"No, Grant, you take this fella into town to a doctor. I'll pay a visit to Vengeance by myself. Besides, one man will be more likely to get inside this 'armed camp' that he called it easier that two," Brent said nodding in Wallace's direction.

They loaded Wallace into the back of the wagon along with Dobbs and the other dead man's body and as Brent turned to leave, Wallace gave him a piece of advice.

"Say, Sackett...if you come in from the east side of the ranch house you'll have a lot better cover. Don't try entering from the south though. There's no where to hide. And let me warn you, there'll be lookouts posted."

Brent nodded and grinned slightly, "Thanks, I appreciate that."

"I hope you get Yancey. Plug him one time for me," Wallace said.

Brent nodded and told Grant to take off. Once Grant had gone Brent saddled his horse and told

Mrs. Keeling that he'd be back sometime after sunup.

"Should something happen, though, and I'm not, tell Grant to hitch up the horses and head for Lordsburg. I'll catch up later," Brent said preparing her as to what to do should something happen to him.

She looked at him with a caring gaze and then kissed him on the cheek.

"Be careful, Brent. Don't do anything foolish. You have people who care a great deal about you," she said.

Brent smiled and nodded his head in agreement, "I've come to care a great deal about you all too. Even Dobbs, now that he's gone. I guess he was an all right guy after all."

"I'll pray for your safe return, Brent," Mrs. Keeling said.

"I'll need it."

Brent mounted up and rode off into the night. His next stop would be the Vengeance ranch. He had committed the directions that Wallace had given him to memory and rode at an easy gallop until he found the trail that would lead him to the eastern section of the Vengeance ranch.

Brent reined his horse to a halt on a distant hilltop that gave him a good view of the Vengeance ranch house and barn yard. He dismounted and looked back towards the east. The sky was still dark, but would soon begin to lighten.

Brent didn't want to attempt to enter the ranch house area once the sun began to break through the darkness so he would have to hurry. Off to his right he saw his best avenue of entry; a dry wash with good cover.

Brent mounted up and reined his horse in the direction of the dry creek bed. There were no rocks so the sound of Brent's horse's hooves were greatly muffled. He held a steady gallop until he was within two hundred yards of the barn.

Tying his horse to some underbrush limbs, Brent went to within fifty yards of the barn on foot. He lay behind a cactus plant and scoured the area. He spotted three guards, but also saw a way to the back of the barn that was almost completely concealed from their view.

Hurrying towards the back of the barn Brent climbed between the fence rails of a large corral and to a small back door in the barn. Fortunately the barn door was unlatched and he was able to slip inside the barn unnoticed.

The barn had five stalls on each side and a buckboard at one end. There was a hayloft and a number of barrels and crates stacked near the two large front doors.

Just as Brent reached the front doors he heard footsteps just on the other side and took cover behind several crates. The doors opened and two men came inside the barn.

One of the men pulled a bottle of whiskey from his shirt and handed it to the other man.

"Here, have a shot of this," the man with the bottle said with a laugh.

"Where'd you get this?" the second man wanted to know.

"It's some of Vengeance's private stock. He had me and Joel cleaning out his storeroom the other day and he had almost two full cases of this stuff. I took a bottle and so did Joe."

"You two sure like to live dangerous, I'll say that," the man said and took a long swig from the bottle.

"Hey, when you've got as much whiskey and wine as Vengeance you ain't going to miss a couple of bottles once in awhile. Hurry up and take another swig then give me the bottle back. I don't want Judd to look out and not see us pulling guard duty," the first man said.

The second man took another healthy swig and handed the bottle back to his friend, who also took a couple of large swallows and then slipped the bottle back under his coat.

The two men went back out through the big front doors of the barn and one went to the right and the other to the left. Brent moved up to the doorway and watched the two men until he saw his chance to make it to a haystack without being seen.

Brent sprinted across the open area on the balls of his feet in order to keep his boot heels from being heard. Once at the haystack he was able to move to a wagon that was parked near the house, still without fear of being seen.

Even though the shadows were being quickly lightened due to the rising of the sun, Brent was still able to move up to the side of the house where he found a back door unlatched.

He slipped inside and found himself in the kitchen. He knew that someone would be coming in before long to start fixing breakfast. He had to work fast if he was to do what had to be done and then try to escape.

Guns of Vengeance Valley

As he moved towards the door that led from the kitchen to the large dining room, he heard voices. The voices belonged to a man and a woman. Looking around Brent saw that the only place he could hide was in a storage area with a curtain across the front of it.

He just got behind the curtain and pulled it closed when the couple entered the kitchen. It was Judd Vengeance and his wife, Edna and they arguing over Towanda.

"I don't care what you say, Edna, nothing is going on between Towanda and me. She said that her window was stuck and asked me to free it. That's the only reason I was in her room," Judd Vengeance said angrily.

"Judd, don't take me for a fool. I've known for several years that you and that winch were having an affair. But at least then you kept it secret. Now you're flaunting it in my face and making me look like a fool. I'll not stand for it. Either she goes, or I do," Mrs. Vengeance said with finality in her tone.

"If you go, you'll leave all this. The ranch, the wealth I've built up over the years, everything," Judd threatened.

"I think a good lawyer would see to it that I got what was coming to me," Edna replied.

"You'd better be very careful woman, or I'll see to it that you get what's coming to you," Judd snapped back.

"Are you threatening me, Judd?"

"Yes, I guess I am. If you try to take what I've worked all my life to attain away from me, you'd better believe I'm threatening you. No one will ever take all this away from me," Judd said, his voice trembling from anger.

Edna's eyes widened as she stared into her husband's face and saw the rage contorting it. She had never actually feared her husband, but he had been showing more and more disrespect for her and her feelings lately and she could see that his callousness was only getting worse as he got older.

Chapter
19

Just then another man's voice broke into the conversation. It was Jack Yancey. Brent listened intently as the two men talked about what had happened in front of Edna Vengeance.

"I'm afraid you lost a couple of your men, Judd," Yancey said when he entered the room.

"Jack, haven't I told you to knock before you enter this house," Judd snapped.

"Why, you're with your wife this time," Yancey answered.

Edna glared at her husband and then at Yancey.

"What do you mean I lost a couple of men? Did you take care of this Brent Sackett or not?"

"My gun jammed after I fired one shot and I had to take it on the lam," Yancey lied.

"What happened to Wallace and Gordy? They're not dead are they?" Vengeance asked in a stern voice.

"I don't know if they are or not. I just told you I had to high tail it out of there when my gun jammed. I think Wallace was alive, but I can't swear to it," Yancey said and then looked towards the storage area where Brent was hiding.

Fortunately Brent was peering through a slit in the parted curtain and when he noticed Yancey look his way and then glance down at the floor realized his boots must be sticking out from under the drapery.

Yancey went for his gun but didn't stand a chance as Brent pulled and fired through the curtain; his bullet catching Yancey in the stomach. Yancey went up on his toes as he grabbed his belly and fired one shot into the kitchen floor.

The suddenness of the gunplay took Vengeance by surprise and by the time he reacted to it, Brent had fired another round and finished Yancey off. Vengeance continued going for his gun, but Brent turned his gun on him and fired one shot that hit Vengeance in the shoulder.

Judd's gun went flying from his hand and skittered across the floor. He grabbed his shoulder and then glared at Brent as he grimaced in pain.

"You'd be Brent Sackett, I take it?"

"You'd be right. I don't appreciate anyone sending three bushwhackers to kill me, Vengeance. Now I want you to call off your men or I'll do to you what you sent Yancey to do to me," Brent snapped angrily.

"My men will cut you down like a rabid coyote, Sackett," Vengeance growled.

"If they do you'll go down with me," Brent said and looked towards the sound of voices outside that were drawing closer.

"Shoot him," Edna Vengeance said to Brent. "They won't have any reason to harm you if he's dead," she went on.

Guns of Vengeance Valley

Not only did Judd look shocked at Edna's statement, but so did Brent. The woman meant it; she wanted her husband dead.

From outside the back door someone yelled out, "Are you okay, Mr. Vengeance?"

"It's Sackett, kill..." Judd started to say just before Brent hit him over the head with his pistol, knocking him unconscious.

"Don't worry, I'll call them off," Edna said as she moved towards the door.

Yelling out as loud as she could she said, "It's all right, boys. We're just having another one of our arguments."

"What were the gunshots about," the man called back.

"Judd killed Jack Yancey. He attacked Judd and Judd had to kill him," Edna replied.

"Boss, are you all right?" the man called out, not trusting what he was being told by Mrs. Vengeance.

Edna looked quickly at Brent and nodded for him to answer. Brent put his hand to his mouth and said a muffled, "Yeah, I'm okay."

The man hesitated for a moment and then asked, "What do you want us to do?"

"Judd was hit in the mouth, Hank; that's why he can't talk right now. He wants you boys to go back to your posts," Edna said.

There was some mumbling amongst the men outside as they began to disburse. Just then Towanda entered the kitchen and stopped short when she saw Yancey lying on the floor. Then she saw Judd and put her hand to her mouth as she stifled a scream.

143

"He's not dead, Towanda," Edna said with a deep frown. "I wish he was, but he's not."

Towanda looked at Brent and then at Edna and asked, "What is the meaning of all this? Did Judd kill Yancey...or did he?" she said looking at Brent.

"He did, thank God. Hell will burn a little hotter now," Edna snapped.

Towanda started to kneel down by Judd, but Edna quickly moved up to where she was and bent down and picked Judd's pistol and pointed it at Towanda.

"I want you out of this house within the hour, do you hear me?"

Towanda's eyes flashed from anger to fear as she looked at the gun in Edna's hand. She wanted to argue but was too frightened to do so. Although she did manage a feeble, "Judd will be angry when he comes too."

"He may become angry, but you'll be gone. Now get back upstairs and start packing," Edna ordered.

Towanda backed out of the room and then ran towards the stairs. Brent looked at Edna and thought for a moment she might turn the gun on him, but she didn't.

Instead she went to the kitchen window and peered through the drawn curtains. The men were all going back to their respective positions around the ranch house and barnyard.

"We'll have to figure a way to get you out of here safely...Mr. Sackett, isn't it?" Edna said.

"Yes, ma'am, Sackett...why are you helping me this way?" Brent asked.

"Because, Mr. Sackett, you've helped me, that's why. You don't know how miserable my life has been living with this man for the last twenty years. He's gotten more and more difficult with each new acquisition. He had visions of being a territorial governor; any territory and setting up what he called a 'Vengeance Empire'. Now you have brought an end to it," she said as she looked down at her husband.

She went on, "And then he brought his mistress into the house as our live in maid. He said it was to make my life easier, but it was so he wouldn't have to make his weekly trips into Lordsburg to the brothel where she worked," Edna said, her words dripping with venom as she looked towards the door that Towanda had gone through earlier.

Edna turned her attention back to Brent and her unconscious husband and said excitedly, "Now we've got to get you out of here."

She knelt down and pulled the corduroy coat off her husband and told Brent to put it on. Then she rushed to the hat rack by the front door and got one of Judd's hats and brought it to Brent to wear.

"Use some of my knitting yarn and tie Judd up and put a gag over his mouth. And while you're doing that I'll go out and have one of the men bring a buckboard around and tell them that I have to take my husband into town to see the doctor and to get the sheriff. Then I'll come back inside and bring you out keeping your head down so they can't recognize you and I'll drive you out of the yard here. Do you have a horse?"

"Yes, it's down in the dry wash behind the barn," Brent replied.

"Good, I'll stop when I get to where the dry wash crosses the road and you can go and get it. I'll go on

145

into town so they will follow me if they should find Judd bound and gagged in the house."

Brent went about tying Judd up and put a gag in his mouth. By the time he had finished Edna was back and they waited for the ranch hand to bring the buckboard around. Since Brent and Judd were about the same size it was easy to mistake Brent for Judd especially wearing his coat and hat.

The man who brought the buckboard around was none other than Joel Holbrook. As he moved in to give Mrs. Vengeance a hand getting her husband to the buckboard he caught a good look of the man's face.

Brent looked directly into Joel's face and after a look of complete and total surprise a huge grin covered his old friend's face. He didn't say a word, just continued to grin and chuckle lightly to himself.

Once in the buckboard Edna drove out of the yard and headed for the point where the road crossed the dry wash. Brent was taken by total surprise at how much she was helping him with his escape and couldn't help but question why. She had explained it somewhat, but there was more to it, he felt.

When they reached the dry wash Edna pulled the team of horses to a halt and said, "Go, hurry before they find Judd."

Brent thanked her when he got out and then ran down the dry creek bed to where his horse was tied. He mounted up and kicked the horse into a full gallop. By now the sun had cleared the eastern mountain range and the landscape was awash in sunlight.

Brent knew that it would just be a matter of time before Judd Vengeance and a dozen men would be on his trail. He had to get Mrs. Keeling and the others into Lordsburg where they would be safe. He would worry about dealing with Vengeance once he knew they were out of Harm's way.

Raymond D. Mason

Chapter 20

Lordsburg, NM

Brent looked at Mrs. Keeling and said, "I want you and the kids to stay in the hotel no matter what you might hear. There's going to be a lot of shooting I'm sure so keep down and don't go to the window to look out."

"Maybe he won't come looking for you," Mrs. Keeling said.

"He'll come, I'm sure of that. Just do as I say. I've told the sheriff and he has got a couple of deputies who will give me a hand...or so he says anyway," Brent replied.

"Brent, I want to know why you won't let me give you a hand," Grant Holt questioned with a deep frown.

"Grant it's better if I handle this thing alone. I'm used to it. I have more experience working this way than I do working with others. I'll be moving so fast that I'm afraid no one else could keep up," Brent stated.

Grant didn't argue, but figured that he would give Brent some cover without Brent even being aware of it. He'd find a place atop one of the buildings where he would have a bird's eye view of the street below. One thing was sure; he wasn't going to let Brent do this all by himself.

It was just before eleven o'clock in the morning when Brent saw ten riders entering Lordsburg from the direction of the Vengeance ranch. The deputies the sheriff had promised were no shows. It appeared Brent was alone in this.

Grant Holt, however, had taken his Winchester and a box of shells atop the hotel roof and had a good view of the street below. He saw Brent standing between two buildings on the opposite side of the street. Brent didn't see Grant, however.

Brent figured the lead rider would be Judd Vengeance, but it wasn't; it was Joel Holbrook. In fact, Judd Vengeance was no where to be seen. Following the men on horseback was the buckboard that Edna Vengeance had used to get Brent to safety. Edna was driving it.

Brent stepped out into the street in front of Joel and hoped he wasn't making himself an easy target. Joel held up his hand and the riders all stopped behind him.

"Say, Brent," Joel said.

"Say, Joel...what's this all about?" Brent asked.

"It looks like its over. Judd Vengeance is dead," Joel said and looked back towards the buckboard.

"Dead...I didn't kill him when I hit him with my gun did I?" Brent questioned.

Joel shook his head negatively and said, "No, Edna shot him with his own gun."

Brent looked shocked as Joel went on.

Guns of Vengeance Valley

"We all saw what happened and she had no other choice but to shoot in self defense. It was either him or her."

"What happened?"

"While she was gone getting you off the ranch, Towanda went brought him around and freed him. He grabbed another gun and came outside in a rage. When Edna drove up he began cussing her out and actually raised his gun to shoot her. She had one of his guns on the wagon seat and she shot him in the chest. He's in the wagon back there now," Joel stated.

"Well I'll be...," Brent said.

"We told her we would come in with her as witnesses to her act of self defense," Joel said.

"She certainly saved my bacon, I can tell you that," Brent said.

Just then Bob and Shelah Colton walked out of the hotel and stopped when they saw all the riders.

"I wonder what this is all about," Bob asked his wife.

"I don't know, but look at the initials on the side of that buckboard. It's JV. You don't suppose it stands for Judd Vengeance do you?

Bob said, "Let's go over and ask," she said.

They walked up alongside Brent and got a casual look as Bob Colton asked, "What's going on, a parade?"

Brent looked at Colton, but didn't answer. Joel did, "We brought the body of Judd Vengeance in to the sheriff's office.

"You mean someone killed him?" Bob said in a surprised voice.

Joel nodded his head yes.

151

"Well, there goes a good idea out the window," Bob said and cast a quick look at Shelah.

"Back to Monterey, California it looks like," Shelah said with a slight grin.

"Is that where you folks are going?" Brent asked.

"Yes, it is...why do you ask?" Bob questioned.

"We're headed out there as well. Have you been to Monterey?"

"Yeah, it's a beautiful place," Bob said.

"What about the Sacramento area? Ever been there," Brent questioned.

"Yeah, it ain't no Monterey, but it's all right."

"Monterey is really pretty, huh?" Brent asked again.

"It's one of the most beautiful spots along the California coast," Shelah opined.

"Maybe we'll change our destination," Brent said thoughtfully.

"Well, good luck," Bob said and he and Shelah turned and headed back to the hotel to pack their bags and make the trip back to Tucson for the next leg of their journey.

Bob looked at Shelah and laughed, "I don't know, maybe it wasn't all that great a plan after all, eh honey?"

"Probably not, Bob," Shelah said with her own laugh.

The sheriff came out of his office and listened to what Joel and the other riders for the Vengeance ranch had to say and then told Mrs. Vengeance that she was free to go, that no charges would be filed against her.

Brent watched her turn the buckboard around and head back down the road in the direction of the ranch. Eight of the riders rode back with her, the other three had decided to move on to greener pastures.

Joel was one of those who returned to the ranch. It was obvious that the ones who had ridden into town with Mrs. Vengeance were working cowhands. That meant that all the hired guns Vengeance had brought in had already gone.

Now it was time for Brent and his traveling companions to get back on the trail to California. Their next stop would be Tucson, Arizona. Now Grant would have to drive Dobbs's wagon. Hopefully the going would be easier from this point on.

The End

Look for the next edition in the Sackett series entitled, "Seven Guns to the Border".

Books by This Author

Mysteries

8 Seconds to Glory - A Motive for Murder - A Tale of Tri-Cities - A Walk on the Wilder Side – Beyond Missing - Blossoms in the Dust - Brotherhood of the Cobra – Counterfeit Elvis: Welcome to My World – Corrigan - If Looks Could Kill - Illegal Crossing - In the Chill of the Night - Most Deadly Intentions – Murder on the Oregon Express - Odor in the Court - On a Lonely Mountain Road - Return of 'Booger' Doyle - Send in the Clones - Shadows of Doubt - Sleazy Come, Sleazy Go - Suddenly, Murder - The Mystery of Myrtle Creek - The Secret of Spirit Mountain - The Tootsie Pop Kid - The Woman in the Field - Too Late To Live

Raymond D. Mason

<u>Westerns</u>

Aces and Eights - Across the Rio Grande – Between Heaven and Hell - Beyond the Great Divide - Beyond the Picket Wire - Brimstone; End of the Trail - Day of the Rawhiders - Four Corners Woman – Guns of Vengeance Valley - Incident at Medicine Bow - King of the Barbary Coast - Laramie - Last of the Long Riders - Man from Silver City – Moon Stalker - Night of the Blood Red Moon - Night Riders - Purple Dawn - Rage at Del Rio - Range War - Rebel Pride - Return to Cutter's Creek - Ride the Hard Land - Ride the Hellfire Trail - Showdown at Lone Pine - Streets of Durango: *Lynching* - Streets of Durango: *Shootings* - Tales of Old Arizona - The Long Ride Back - Three Days to Sundown - Yellow Sky, Black Hawk

**Go to www.createspace.com and use L9ZJ9ZJJ 'discount code' for 30% off.
<u>Books are also on Kindle</u>.**

7

Printed in Great Britain
by Amazon